INTO THE LABYRINTH

DREAMWEAVERS BOOK 2

ISA PEARL RITCHIE

TE RĀ
AROHA
PRESS

First published 2020

© Isa Pearl Ritchie 2020

ISBN 978-0-473-50547-9

A catalogue record for this book is available from the National
Library of New Zealand

TE RĀ AROHA PRESS

This book is dedicated to the Grove of the Summer Stars, the Order of Bards, Ovates and Druids...

...and all the children who dream of other worlds

THE DR

THE

THE MOUNTAINS

THE DESER

THE BAY

PROLOGUE

*I*t might look as if Awa is sleeping soundly, wrapped in her duvet, but inside her mind, a part of her is very much awake, and if we can follow it, we'll find her splashing around in a lake.

Not just any lake – a purple lake, reflecting the colour of the swirling sky above. We can see her splashing, and talking to a small glowing creature, floating on the shore. She's calling out to this creature, Veila, showing her how she is starting to shape the water splashes into patterns. For, you see, Awa is a Dreamweaver, in training, learning to master her powers in the wonderful Dreamrealm. If we zoom out just a little bit, we can see mountains in the distance and a large forest to the edge of the lake. We can pan over this forest and find the Grove of trees that marks Awa's safe entrance into the Dreamrealm, and further towards a vast, wide, rolling meadow, and off to the inky indigo coloured sea.

Somewhere in the meadow, we find the Priestess Tree, big, and strong and wise, and just to her left, we see what remains of a giant dome, that at one stage covered the entire tree and some of the area around.

The large glass dome, that Awa valiantly trapped the shadow fragments in, now sits quietly... or does it? From the outside, the glass looks fogged up, so that nothing can be seen. Anything could be lurking in there, planning its escape, or worse. If we rest here, just a moment too long, we might notice a disturbance in the fog inside. We might feel a tingle of fear dancing up our spines just before we are startled by the palm of a hand as it hits the inside of the dome. It disappears and underneath we both swear we saw eyes looking out at us, blinking... and just then, we hear a cracking noise, quiet at first, but growing louder.

CHAPTER ONE

"Well, that wasn't as bad as I thought," Ella said, smiling at me as we walked to the courtyard at lunchtime. "The teachers made it sound like it was going to be a really hard test."

"It was pretty bad," said Evan, swinging his bag down so it hung over the front of his yellow hoodie. "For me, at least! But spelling is not really my thing."

I laughed. "It's not really my thing either," I said. "I mean, isn't that what autocorrect is for?"

My friends laughed as we sat down at our usual table.

"Anyone want to swap for this amazing peanut butter sandwich?" Evan asked; he was always trying to swap his lunch.

My normal waking life was so different compared to my dreams these days – which had become a whole other life of their own.

I watched my friends argue about the value of

peanut butter sandwiches. Their heads tipped towards each other; Ella's light brown bob almost as straight at Evan's black hair, and both of them happened to be wearing yellow today, so they looked like a matching set.

I wonder if I'll ever be able to tell them about the Dreamrealm.

It seemed like years since I first discovered the Dreamrealm when really it had only been a few months. I didn't know there was such a thing as a 'sensitive' before the Veila, the dreamcharmer, turned up in my room one night and told me I was one. I'd never heard of Dreamweavers either, but apparently, that's what I am.

It feels like a big responsibility to be the first Dreamweaver in years, but I don't mind as long as it means I get to keep going to the Dreamrealm where the colours are brighter and where I feel most at home – although it was also where, just weeks ago, I was attacked by some very unusual characters.

I'd thought that would be the end of me, but I managed to trap them and get out and since then everything had been peaceful and beautiful again. I know there are still risks, and there are some very cryptic clues that I have to figure out to master my Dreamweaver powers...

An image swam back into my mind of the visions shown to me by the Priestess Tree: *a handful of special stones, the dark tunnels of the underground labyrinth. I have to find them!*

Ella looked at me. "Isn't everything better than it was just a few weeks ago?"

"What?" I asked. "Oh, yeah." I smiled. Of course she wasn't talking about the Dreamrealm. "So much better!" I said.

I know I can't tell them. It's too risky – they'll think I'm crazy!

"Yeah," Evan said. "It's like a whole different world since you stood up to Felicity."

"Well that's the thing," I said, remembering all the bullying when I first started at Magnolia Heights Intermediate earlier in the year. "I didn't really stand up to her – it was just…"

"Well, she went way too far," Ella said. "It made sense that your mum put her on the spot like that."

I blushed, remembering how awkward it had been – Mum making the principal get Felicity to apologise in front of everyone for those awful pink posters – with Evan and I in a love heart after Felicity found my note telling Evan I didn't like him. *I bet she knew,* I thought. *I bet she knew Ella likes Evan and she was trying to hurt her as well.*

I looked back over at my friends, doing exaggerated impressions of Felicity and of Ms Norton, the principal. I wondered whether Ella would ever tell Evan how she felt about him. *Probably not,* I thought, *but maybe they could figure it out somehow…*

Just then I heard a strange sound coming from overhead. I looked up.

"What is it, Awa?" Ella asked.

"That cracking noise," I said. "Can you hear it?"

I looked back at my friend's blank faces.

"No," they both said, at the same time, and smiled at each other.

"Never mind," I said. "It's probably nothing."

I tried to push my worries out of my mind. *It's probably nothing...* I picked up my own peanut butter sandwich and found that it was pretty good.

CHAPTER TWO

That night I closed my eyes and counted my breathing in: *one, two, three, four*. Then out: *one, two, three, four, five, six*. I did this three times, and by the time I had finished, as usual, I was feeling pretty sleepy. Then I recited the charm that Veila had given me to get back to the Grove in the Dreamrealm:

> *I am water, earth, sun and sky.*
> *I am dawn, noon, dusk and midnight.*
> *I am the whisper in the wind...*
> *and I am here.*

I could hear the sound of the stream before I opened my eyes to see the trees of the Grove all around me. I felt light and safe and relaxed. Being here was so unlike anywhere in the waking world. I lay in the soft thick grass and looked up at the bushy trees surrounding the Grove and the swirling purple sky above, feeling so peaceful. Sure, my waking life had been much easier lately. I hadn't been getting so much anxiety since Felicity had apologised in front of the whole school for bullying. She hadn't spoken to me since then, which was just fine by me. But even though my parents were being nice and school was okay and it was great hanging out with my friends, nothing was quite as relaxing as coming here.

"Awa!"

Veila's yell jolted me out of my relaxation.

"What?" I asked.

"Get up," she said, floating above me. Her small, glowing form looked oddly like a peachy coloured lamp blowing in the wind.

"Why?" I asked. "I was actually enjoying just relaxing here, listening to the stream."

"We don't have *time* for relaxing," Veila said. "We have training to do!"

I sighed.

"Come on Awa, the Shadow isn't resting – you shouldn't either!"

I looked at Veila, recognising the fear in her voice – the same fear that I heard any time the Shadow came up in conversation.

"Not this stuff about the Shadow again," I said. "I don't even understand what it is."

"Awa," Veila said, visibly trembling. "You know the Shadow is connected to those awful fragments who attacked us. Judgement and the Politician are big shadow fragments, and you know they haven't disappeared. They're still in that dome you trapped them in, and they won't stay there forever."

"Fine," I said and got up. *So now I can't get any rest, even in my dreams!*

"I have a new idea," Veila said, pacing back and forth in the air in a way that better suited a military general than a dreamcharmer.

"What is it?" I asked.

"Well, last time, we were practising with the water."

"Making pretty splashes!" I recalled. "That was fun."

"It doesn't always have to be fun," Veila said, solemnly. I wondered if she was worried about the fragments coming back – the ones we trapped in the glass dome – or was it something else?

"So, what then?" I asked, trying to take her more seriously.

"You need to learn to use your Dreamweaver powers," Veila said. "This is so important. We never know when you might really need them."

I sighed. "Yeah, I know. What do you have in mind?"

"The Priestess Tree told me that there are no limits on your powers, the only limits are in how you have learnt – or not learnt – to use them."

"So you're saying I can do anything?" I asked.

"No, you *could* do anything if you could be bothered figuring out how," Veila said, crossing her arms, "but if you don't keep trying you will never get to the kind of mastery required to alchemise the fragments."

I shivered, remembering how awful some of the

fragments had been, especially the Politician and Judgement, who had tried to sap all the life out of me – tried to steal my power. They wanted to be in control of the Dreamrealm. The Politician wanted to build big stadiums to give his speeches and Judgement wanted to make giant ballrooms, and get rid of all the trees. Even though I'd trapped them, I knew they were still there under that dome, and they would probably try to get out and do it all over again. It was only by pure luck that I had managed to trick them into looking into the mirror that Honu, the giant turtle, had found for me at the bottom of the lake.

It had turned out that the fragments' greatest weakness was their fascination with their own reflection. *They're probably still exactly where we left them,* I thought, *squabbling over the mirror, and they're trapped by the glass dome anyway.* But I knew that eventually I would have to face them again.

"Okay, okay," I said, getting up. "What do you want to try?"

"According to the Priestess Tree, you have the power to bend and shape things – anything," Veila said. "So I thought we could try focusing on your hands."

"My hands?" I looked down. "My hands look fine," I said, although they were glowing a little bit.

"Yes, sure, they're fine, but I want you to imagine a ball of energy in them," Veila said. "Cup your hands together and close your eyes."

I sighed and did as I was told. I knew Veila was only

trying to help. I could tell she was worried, and it made me uncomfortable.

I tried to focus on my hands, but I didn't feel anything changing. I kept getting distracted by the sound of the stream, which made me want to lie down in the grass again. I thought about Ella and wondered what she was dreaming about right now... maybe she was dreaming about Evan. I wondered if they were both in the House of Mind, in separate rooms – or even in the same room but in separate dimensions, in their own fantasy worlds – coming so close but never seeing each other.

"Awa?" Veila said.

"Sorry... I'm trying," I lied. I had actually totally forgotten about what we were doing for a moment.

"Let's try again," Veila said. "Open your eyes this time."

I opened my eyes and looked at the palms of my cupped hands.

"Now try to imagine the energy swirling around," Veila said. "Give it a colour – like orange."

"Orange?" I said. "Does it have to be?"

"What's wrong with orange?" Veila asked.

"Mum likes orange," I said.

"You humans are so strange," Veila replied. "Give it whatever colour you like, just imagine it – the energy – swirling around in your hand."

I tried to imagine blue light swirling in my hands, but nothing happened. I tried again and again but nothing I did seemed to work.

"This is impossible!" I said, and lay back down on the grass.

"It's not at all impossible," Veila said. "What a silly concept!"

"It's not working," I argued.

"You just need to focus," Veila assured me.

CHAPTER THREE

"*I*'m tired," I said to Veila. I had been in the grove for ages, trying and failing to use my Dreamweaver powers. "I've had enough, can't we do something easy?"

"Easy?" Veila asked.

"Yeah – something fun. Can't we do more exploring? I'm pretty sure there is heaps more of the Dreamrealm to see!"

It was Veila's turn to sigh. "Okay," she said, "but we are going to try this again tomorrow."

"Isn't it funny," I said, lying back down in the Grove, "...how everyone speaks English here?"

"No one speaks English here," Veila replied.

"What? So what do you speak then?"

"We speak in meaning – obviously. We speak in feelings and understanding and intuition. You just hear it as English because it's what you're used to."

"How strange."

"You are really quite strange," said Veila, staring at me as if I was an alien.

"Hey, Veila. Do you remember what the Priestess Tree showed me – a while ago? There were a handful of special stones and the seacliffs?"

"Did she?" Veila said, absentmindedly running her fingers over a blade of grass.

"Do you think if we go there – to the seacliffs, we might find something... maybe a clue about the stones or the Labyrinth?"

"We can try," Veila said.

We made our way out of the Grove and into the meadow because Veila had some kind of rule about not flying out of the Grove, directly. I crouched down and then propelled myself into the air, rising higher into the purple sky. Clouds of pink jellyfish and blue butterflies darted out of my way, and the island below seemed to open up as I rose higher and higher.

Veila darted all around me. She was so much faster than I was that it made me feel a bit slow and clumsy, even though I was flying through the air!

I looked out in the direction of the seacliffs. I could see the shape of familiar birds, circling in the distance. The gulls!

As we drew closer, the gulls came in to land near the cliffs. I dropped down onto the ground beside them.

"Hello!" I said, happy to see these wonderful birds, who had helped me escape the Politician and Judgement who were sapping me of my powers, almost destroying the entire Dreamrealm.

"Greetings, Dreamweaver," said the largest gull.

"I didn't really get to thank you for all your help – rescuing me from the fragments," I said.

"We do what we can," he replied. "You don't need to thank us. It was part of our role here."

"Okay," I said. "I have a question… about this place. The Priestess Tree showed me it in a vision, but I don't know why… was it just that you were supposed to help me earlier on, or is there some other clue here?"

"What clue do you seek?"

"I'm trying to find the Labyrinth," I said.

The enormous bird looked me directly in the eye and said, "What you seek is hiding in plain sight, but you must retrace your steps to find it."

"What?" I asked.

"That is all I can tell you," the gull said.

I sighed.

"Why is it that no one gives me clear answers around here?!"

"There are no instructions to life, Dreamweaver. We are all here, learning and growing. Nothing is clear until we do the work to understand it."

"What about the stones?" I asked.

"What stones?" the gull said. "There are plenty of stones around here, if you're interested in them."

I looked out at rocky cliffs and stones below.

"Sure there are plenty of stones, but none of them

look anything like the ones the Priestess Tree showed me, which were shiny and in bright colours."

"You possess the power to transform things, Dreamweaver," the gull reminded me.

"I'm sure I do," I said, "if only I knew how to use it! And it seems like I can't learn because I need the powers first – it all just goes around in circles!"

"It was good to see you, friend," the gull said. "And now we take our leave." He bowed and took off into the sky, followed by the other gulls.

What I seek is hiding in plain sight...

I couldn't see anything but the indigo coloured ocean and the purple, swirling sky. I turned back towards the land. To my left, the land stretched out towards a sandy bay, with the mountains in the distance. The lush meadow spread out in front of me, with the Priestess Tree, and the Rooms of Mind, with forest behind everything, and to the right, along the coastline, I could just make out the tall Elisiad Tree, which stretched up towards the sky. I remembered the taste of the sweet Elisiad berries which had helped me to come back to the Dreamrealm… but I couldn't see anything that led me closer to the Labyrinth.

CHAPTER FOUR

I woke up with the sound of the Dreamrealm sea fresh in my mind. I thought of how much Ella would love meeting the giant seagulls, being such a big fan of animals. *I wish I could tell her about the Dreamrealm.*

I was waiting for Mum to come and hassle me about getting up for school, but then I remembered it was Saturday!

I rolled over in bed, trying to think of a way I could tell Ella that would make sense... *Maybe I can just tell her a little bit at a time, to test how much she believes me, then I can keep adding things in until I can tell her the whole thing.*

I checked my phone and saw there was a notification: a new video from Valerie Sparkles!

I pressed play. Valerie Sparkles appeared with her pink and purple hair, and her very cool makeup.

"Have I got a surprise for you!?" she said, in her

American accent. She pulled out a small glittery cylinder, and held it up, twisting it so it sparkled.

"This is my new – fabulous – lip gloss!" she said. "It's 100% cruelty-free, and it will keep your lips nice and soft. And that's not the best part: it comes in ten different shades of pink and purple! Oh, and did I mention that it GLOWS IN THE DARK?!"

Awesome!

I watched as she applied the purple sparkly gloss to her already purple sparkly lips and turned off the light. All I could see were her lips, glowing in the dark.

So cool.

"Awa," Mum said. "You're up early."

"I need this!" I said, jumping up and holding my phone up to Mum's face.

Mum frowned. "What is it?"

"It's AMAZING lip gloss! It's sparkly and comes in ten different shades and it GLOWS IN THE DARK!"

"What do you need glow in the dark lips for?" Mum asked, raising her eyebrow.

"Because I do!" I said.

"It sounds like a big waste of money," Mum said. "How much does it cost?"

I looked down at my phone screen to see the numbers flash up. "39.99," I said, not looking at Mum, I added, "US dollars."

"Awa!" Mum said. "That's an outrageous price for lip balm!"

"It's lip *gloss*," I said, "not balm."

"Still," Mum said, shaking her head.

"But it comes in purple!"

"It's still a waste of money!"

I sighed and collapsed on the bed. *Maybe Dad will buy it for me,* I thought, but I knew he would think it was a waste of money, too.

I got up and made myself some toast. I was feeling a bit woozy because I hadn't eaten yet. I spread a thick layer of butter and an even thicker layer of chocolate hazelnut spread, careful to hide my plate from Mum so she didn't give me *that* look.

As I ate I thought back to my dream of the gulls and how much Ella would love to meet them.

I have to find a way to tell her, I thought. It was getting too hard to keep my two lives separate. Out here in the waking world I had no one to talk to about the Dreamrealm.

I had barely finished my toast before I called Ella.

"Hello?" her face popped up on the screen.

"Hi!" I said, walking to my room with the phone and closing the door behind me.

"Oh my god, Awa," Ella said. Her face was glowing. "You'll never guess what happened?"

"What?" I asked her. "What happened?"

"So, Evan rang me last night!" Ella said, her voice rising to a squeak.

"He did?" I asked.

"Yes!" Ella said. "He rang me and said that he likes me! HE LIKES ME!"

"Wow," I said.

I wanted to feel happy for Ella, because I knew she

had liked Evan for ages, but something else was happening inside me. I tried to smile into the screen.

"Isn't this great?" Ella asked.

"Yeah," I said, trying to look like I meant it.

"He likes me," Ella said again, looking like she might implode from joy.

"Really great!" I said, trying to sound as enthusiastic as I could. I couldn't explain what was going on inside me, but it wasn't good. I decided to just get on with what I had called Ella for, anyway.

"So, do you want to hang out later today?" I asked. Maybe I would feel better by then. Maybe I could still find a way to tell Ella about the Dreamrealm, though for some reason it seemed less important now.

"Oh, Awa!" Ella said. "I can't… I mean, I can hang out a bit but… I think we have a date!"

"A… date?" I asked.

"Evan asked me if I wanted to go out to a movie with him!" Ella looked a bit worried now. "Maybe you could come over and help me decide what to wear?"

"Uhh, actually," I said, thinking fast, "I've just remembered I have to do something with my dad later. Maybe another time?"

I couldn't think of anything worse than watching Ella try on outfits and stress about how she looked. It would be just like a whole lot of weekends that I'd spent with my old friend Melody from my last school, who I didn't really talk to anymore because we had nothing in common. *Is that what I'm worried about?* I wondered. *Is that why I feel this way? Am I scared that my friends will go off and hang out without me and we will end up having nothing in common?*

I sighed.

"Are you alright, Awa?" Ella asked.

"Me?" I said, plastering on a smile. "Yes, of course I am. Just a bit tired."

"What about Sunday?" Ella asked.

"Sunday?"

"Yeah, we could hang out on Sunday."

"Oh," I said. "Maybe, I'll have to check with Mum." I looked up, towards my closed door. "I've got to go now," I said, as if Mum was waving to me.

"Okay," Ella said.

"But I'm happy for you. I hope you both have a great time!" I hung up the phone and lay down on the bed.

Do I really hope that? I wondered. *No,* came the answer. *But don't I want my friends to be happy? Of course I do... So what's going on?*

I shoved my head into a pillow, as if it was a sponge, trying to soak up some of the weird feelings going through me. *I want to be happy for Ella, maybe I'm just scared that my two friends will start spending all their time together and I'll be left out.*

It's not a big deal, I told myself. *It's not going to happen that way. Things will be fine.* But somehow I didn't believe that.

CHAPTER FIVE

I tried to avoid thinking about Ella and Evan for the rest of the day. I watched a whole lot of old Valerie Sparkles videos online until Mum told me I'd had enough 'screen time', so I did some drawing instead.

I drew Valerie Sparkles, with her pink and purple hair, only I left out the pink because it's not my thing. I drew her in front of the sea, looking out towards an island, because I know how to draw islands up on the horizon, and the patterns that water makes.

Everyone watches Valerie Sparkles. I wonder how she got so popular, with her unusual hair and style.

She had started off by making videos about the newest games – she would play them and review them, but then she started making videos about everything – even why the sky is blue! My favourite ones were where she talked about real things that had gone on in her life, like when her parents divorced. Somehow she was just like me. She was much stranger than most of the other kids I knew who also watched her videos. Most of them wouldn't even want to have purple hair. *I would, if only Mum and Dad would let me!*

The Valerie in my picture looked back at me. I had drawn her a serious face, but then tried to change it to a smile. She looked sad – like she was just pretending to smile. *I know the feeling.*

I went to bed that night with a heavy feeling in my chest. *Anxiety again*, with all its familiar messages: *there's something wrong with me. Why can't I keep friends? Why don't I get crushes like normal people? Is that why this thing with Ella and Evan is really bothering me – because I'm some kind of freak? My friends don't really like me; they never did. Now they just like each other. I'm going to be alone – forever.* I was at the point of wishing I could just disappear – but at least I could go into the Dreamrealm and escape.

I turned off the light, closed my eyes, counted my breathing to slow it down, and repeated Veila's charm.

I am water, earth, sun, and sky...

I imagined myself as all the things, as I repeated the words in my mind.

...and I am here.

I opened my eyes to find myself in the Grove again, the sound of the flowing stream washing my worries away. *What a relief it is to come here!* I thought.

I walked around the Grove, looking at the pool in the centre. The river flowed through, but the pool somehow stayed as still and smooth as glass. I sat on one of the boulders surrounding the pool and looked around at the wildflowers and berry shrubs growing low to the ground. My eyes came to rest on the little kawakawa plant that had appeared a while back – *from the ancestors*, Veila had said. I wondered where the ancestors were in relation to the Dreamrealm. Were they watching over me, watching my every move, or just looking out for important things like danger?

I still didn't understand what the kawakawa plant meant. It wasn't a warning, like the red lantern which had appeared before the Politician and Judgement attacked me. The lantern had disappeared so quickly – it was like Veila said: *Warnings disappear...* but the kawakawa was still here. It was some other kind of message.

It's a native plant, one that my ancestors would have used... maybe I should ask great aunt Rosetta... It wasn't the first time I'd thought of this, but I always seemed to forget.

I felt so peaceful, sitting there in the Grove. I was actually quite relieved Veila wasn't around. I wasn't really in the mood for her to hassle me to do more training.

I looked around the Grove again. I hadn't really paid any attention to the big trees that surrounded it. I counted nine of them. *What kind of trees are they?* I wondered. I had never thought about it before. The trees had narrow, gnarly trunks with spindly bushy branches covered in bright variegated leaves which stood out against the rest of the forest around them. As I concentrated I noticed small round fruits or seeds in some of the upper branches.

I lay on the grass in the Grove, peacefully, looking up at the trees and wondering if I could climb them to get the fruits – or whether I wouldn't be allowed to. There were more rules around the Grove than other parts of the Dreamrealm. Veila always said I wasn't allowed to fly out of the Grove, I had to go to the meadow instead.

After a while, Veila still hadn't arrived, so I decided to go exploring on my own. I left the Grove and walked along the forest path, out to the meadow.

I wandered through the meadow, enjoying the view for a while.

Which way should I go?

I looked around.

In the distance I could see the hill. I stalled. *Should I go to talk to the Priestess Tree?* I had been back since the fragments were trapped, but not by myself, only with Veila. *Maybe this time she can tell me something more...*

I passed the glass dome on my way to the Priestess Tree. It was silent, and so fogged up I couldn't see a thing, but it still gave me the creeps.

I looked up towards the Priestess Tree. I loved the way her roots twisted together, as if they were woven up her trunk, and her branches reached up to the sky like arms.

I noticed a few new wild flowers growing around her base as I approached. They looked a bit like irises, but pure white. They shimmered in the light like pearls. Every now and then, little rainbow sparks flew out of them like tiny fireworks. I had never seen any like that before. The Dreamrealm was always shifting and changing like that.

I got closer and put my hand up against her trunk. I closed my eyes and spoke to the Priestess Tree with my mind.

Priestess Tree... I'm here, it's Awa.

Greetings, Dreamweaver, her voice replied, inside my head. *Come down to see me.*

I relaxed my mind and let it wander down the twisted roots, deep beneath the earth.

Her beautiful face looked like it was carved into the gnarled wood of the tree roots. Her expression was so serene. Her eyes were closed, as usual, as if in meditation. Her hair came down, from the roots of the tree over her head, and stretched out behind her. Her outfit was made out of a thousand tiny tree roots, reaching up like little flames. Her hands rested on her full belly. She was settled against large cushions of soft earth.

I sighed as I looked at her, wishing I could be so relaxed in my waking life.

Welcome, Dreamweaver, her voice sounded in my mind. *You have some questions for me.*

It always freaked me out, how she could read my mind!

Yes, I said, *I have so many questions!*

I didn't even know where to start.

Last time I visited you, you showed me a maze, under the ground... a labyrinth. I want to know how to get there, I said in my mind.

The seacliffs, came her response.

I went to the seacliffs, Veila and I did. We searched all around. We even asked the gulls for help.

The Priestess Tree was silent, as if she was waiting for me to figure it out myself.

I kept going around in circles.

I knew that the Labyrinth was how the last Dreamweaver had trained because Honu had showed me a vision of him, practicing along its dark tunnels. I had only caught a glimpse of it, but I was guessing that whatever was in the Labyrinth was the key to figuring out how to alchemise the fragments – to stop them from coming back, for good. I knew I'd need this sooner or later, because surely the glass dome I managed to trap them in wasn't going to last forever. Plus, there were bound to be other dangerous fragments around the Dreamrealm that I hadn't trapped. I just needed to find the entrance so that I could get into the Labyrinth.

Can you show me again? I asked.

As you wish, Dreamweaver, she replied. She opened her eyes and the disc appeared in front of her belly, like it had last time, and images began to swirl across it.

I caught a glimpse of the Labyrinth, the seacliffs, and a handful of stones. I had seen them before, the last time the Priestess Tree had showed me images, but I didn't know what they meant. The last image was new. It was the figure of a boy, running through the grass. I couldn't make out his face, but there was something familiar about him.

Who is that? I asked. A*nd what does he have to do with any of this?*

All in good time, Dreamweaver, the Priestess Tree said, infuriatingly.

But I need to know more, now, I said. *Veila is trying to get me to train to use my Dreamweaver powers and she's driving me crazy. But I know time is running out. I keep hearing a cracking sound and I'm sure it's the dome. I need whatever is in that labyrinth. I know I need those stones – I need to at least find the entrance!*

The Priestess Tree had showed me a vision of a handful of special stones... I had no idea what they meant but I was guessing they were connected. I just needed some clue about how to get them.

She smiled at me.

When the fruit is ripe, it will naturally fall into your hands, her voice said.

That is exactly what Veila kept telling me. I sighed. After all I had been through they still didn't think I was ready.

All in good time, the Priestess Tree said again, and I felt my mind floating up from the tree. Standing there, in the meadow, looking out towards the sea.

"Awa." I heard my name, and turned to find myself caught in my sheets. I was waking up. Mum was calling me.

CHAPTER SIX

*G*oosebumps prickled the skin of my forearms as I left the comfort of the heated car, ignoring Mum's complaints about my forgotten jacket. My breath rose in white clouds. The smell of woodsmoke drifted from nearby chimneys. I longed to be in front of the fire, back in my old house, before recalling it no longer existed. It felt like the demolition of my old childhood home was crashing in all around and through me, bringing back that heavy pain again.

How long will it be before it all stops hurting so much?

The bell rang, prompting the crowd of school kids in the quad to move in chaotic patterns, like disturbed ants. I joined the disordered queue towards the front doors.

"I wish I could go home." I was shocked to find I'd said these words aloud. My stomach lurched as I recognised Felicity turning towards me.

"Well, I wish you never even existed."

I felt my chest tighten. Felicity had spoken so loudly that others around us gasped.

I just wanted to disappear. Everything around me started going grey.

It was the first time Felicity had spoken to me since she had been made to apologise in front of the whole school for bullying me. I had hoped all of that was over – but apparently not.

I made it through the rest of the day without anything else going wrong. Ella and Evan seemed quieter than usual, and it made me wonder what was going on – did they regret being friends with me now that Felicity was back to her awful behaviour?

I got home from school that afternoon and Mum was still at work, as usual.

The door was open as I walked past her bedroom. Something red caught my eye: her jewellery box.

As a young child I loved going through Mum's rings and necklaces. Each one had a story – like the pearls from her grandmother, or the bright red earrings from some trip she to Hawaii in her 20s. I knew some had come from Dad and I wanted to see if Mum still had those things… the amethyst ring he gave her when they first got together, or the amber bracelet from their first wedding anniversary, or the sapphire earrings that I had helped him choose for her that last year before the divorce.

I could feel my throat tightening, and prickles of tears in the corner of my eyes as I thought about them – those memories. I had to see if they were still there.

I'll kill her if she's thrown them out!

I double checked to make sure Mum wasn't just about to come through the door – but I knew she was unlikely to be home until much later. Then I sneaked into her room and opened the red box.

I picked up a big tangle of necklaces; the pearls were caught up with some silver and gold chains. I couldn't see any of the things from Dad.

They're not here! I thought in alarm, but then the blue shimmer of sapphire caught my eye. It was one of the earrings I had chosen, sitting in the bottom corner of the box.

I rummaged around until I found the other one, and in the process I also caught sight of the amber bracelet, and the amethyst ring was in another corner.

Mine, something inside me said. *I have to have them.*

It made sense. Mum obviously didn't care enough about Dad to make their marriage work. *She doesn't deserve them, and anyway, she doesn't need a reminder of Dad – he just makes her angry.*

I took the jewellery from Dad back to my room and put them in my jewellery box, where they belonged. Then I felt guilty, but not guilty enough to return them. I watched Valerie Sparkles videos to distract myself.

I could put them back and ask Mum for them... I thought, *but then she might realise I've been through her stuff... and what if she doesn't want to give them to me – or worse, what if she remembers and throw them out!*

No, I couldn't ask Mum for them. She would probably just forget they even existed anyway; she was so
busy with work.

I didn't say anything to Mum when she got home. It
was kind of satisfying knowing I had some more things
that belonged to Dad – especially because I hardly ever
saw him anymore. The ache of missing Dad followed
me for the rest of the day. I tried to call him but he was
busy, so I gave up and went to bed.

I drifted into the Dreamrealm and into the Grove.

CHAPTER SEVEN

I had once thought it would be nice for my friends to like each other. I was wrong. I didn't really want to go to school on Monday. I still felt awful after learning about Ella and Evan going on a date, even though I didn't completely understand why. I couldn't shake the feeling that it was because there was something wrong with me. It was kind of like anxiety but deeper and slower than usual.

There was a weight in the pit of my stomach and I knew it was because of what Ella had told me in the weekend. I could see it all play out in my head:

My only two friends just want to spend all their time together. They look at each other with googlie eyes and blush and pretend they have to study just so they can hang out alone. They are so nice about it: "It's not about you," they say, but I'm left out anyway. They ignore me because they are too busy obsessing about each other and they secretly wish I would disappear.

I knew what was coming. Ella would want to find me at school and tell me about the weekend and how things went with Evan. I didn't want to know about it.

I got to school slightly late on purpose. The bell had just rung and I looked down as I walked, just to make sure I avoided Ella and Evan.

I got to class and Ella was already sitting at a desk. She smiled at me. I smiled back but I knew it wasn't a real smile. I spent the morning pretending to be very interested in my maths every time Ella glanced over at me. At morning break I went to the library and hid in the corner, reading a mystery novel set in St Petersburg. I would rather pretend I was a young Russian detective than deal with my own life.

I went back to class when the bell rang. Mr Jasper was handing out notices.

"School camp is in three weeks," he said. "And no – we will not be sleeping in tents this time – not after last year's fiasco."

I had no idea what had happened the year before, but the kids in front of me were telling each other the story rather loudly, about how some kid had sleep-walked into a number of tents in the night and then tried to pee on one of the teachers. That kid had apparently changed to a different school not long after. I wondered if I would do something equally embarrassing during camp and have to leave. The thought seemed like a relief: *I could start again.*

I glanced over at Ella. She wasn't looking at me but she had a sad expression on her face.

Mr Jasper spent a long time talking about the school camp and going through the list of all the things we would need to bring. The other kids seemed excited, but I just wanted to disappear.

When the bell rang for lunch I quickly returned to the library before Ella could catch me.

I wasn't hungry, anyway. I was deeply absorbed in the scene where the detective was walking around the icy city square, piecing together different parts of the mystery, when she caught a glimpse of a hooded figure disappearing between two trees.

"Awa!"

I jumped.

"There you are!"

It was Ella.

I put my book down and looked up at her. I wondered whether she was going to tell me now that we didn't need to be friends anymore or maybe she was going to keep up the act for a while and let me down gently.

"Hi," I said.

"I've been looking everywhere for you," Ella said.

"I've just been reading," I replied.

Ella gave me a funny look.

"Are you avoiding me?" she asked.

I looked down.

"Awa?" she asked.

"Well," I said, "I'm giving you and Evan some space. I'm sure you don't need me being a third wheel."

"Oh Awa!" Ella said. "Really? It's not the same

without you. We were both just sitting there talking about you, wondering where you were."

"Oh," I said.

"Awa, you're not jealous, are you?" Ella asked, with concern in her eyes.

"What?"

"I mean, I know Evan used to like you, and now…"

"It's not that," I said. "How many times do I have to tell you that I don't like Evan?"

"I just wondered if something had changed," Ella said, shrugging.

The librarian came over to us. "Keep it down, girls!" he hissed, and walked away.

"The only thing that's changed," I said, keeping my voice low, "is that I feel kind of… left out… I guess – like you two will just want to hang out with each other and I won't have any friends."

Tears had started spouting from my eyes and I wiped them away quickly.

"Awa, it's not like that," Ella insisted. "It's… well, it's basically just the same as before," Ella blushed.

"What do you mean?" I asked,

"Let me tell you about what happened on Saturday," Ella said. "It was really so awkward!"

And for the first time, I actually wanted to hear.

Ella told me about how she and Evan had hung out and gone to a movie, about how they had barely spoken to each other, about how she had regretted going because it was so awkward, about how even now at school things were a bit weird and she just wished they would go back to normal.

"That makes two of us," I said.

Ella wrapped her arms around me and gave me a big hug. The sleeve of her favourite yellow cardigan stretched back and I saw her teddy bear watch – the one she always tried to hide from the other kids at school in case they teased her.

And just like that, I knew we would still be friends.

CHAPTER EIGHT

I got home from school wanting to have a nap. I needed to check on the dome, to see if the fragments had escaped. My plan was interrupted when I saw the suitcases sitting in the hallway of our apartment. *That's strange, I didn't realise we were going anywhere.*

Stranger still, the suitcases weren't Mum's, and they certainly weren't mine. These looked battered and old, but quite good quality. There was something familiar about them.

I walked down the hall towards the lounge.

"Here she is!" a big warm voice boomed.

"Rosetta!"

And there she was: my wonderful great aunt Rosetta – my grandmother's flamboyant youngest sister. She was dressed, as usual, from head to toe in purple. This time, even her white hair was dyed a bril-

38

liant shade of violet to match. She instantly wrapped me up in a big hug.

"So good to see you!" Rosetta said in her loud and slightly wavering voice. "My, how you've grown since the summer!"

"It's good to see you too, Aunty," I said, and it really was. "I love your hair! Mum's going to freak. I wish she would let me dye my hair purple."

Rosetta had always been my favourite, growing up. Sure I loved Nan, but she was almost the complete opposite of her baby sister. Nan was quiet while Rosetta was loud, Nan was serious while Rosetta was fun and quirky and playful.

"Now, sit down," Rosetta said, "and tell me about your day. How's school?"

"It's okay," I said. "I have a couple of friends – but you know, it's school."

"Is it dreadfully boring?" Rosetta asked as she moved from the lounge to the kitchen, putting the kettle on to boil water while I talked.

"Yeah – sometimes, but it's not all terrible," I tried to think of something interesting to add. "We've got a school camp coming up."

"Oh – how wonderful!" Rosetta said, "School camp – where will that be?"

"Umm, I'm not sure, it's about an hour's drive away… In some mountains, I think… There are cabins and…"

"Mountains," Rosetta said. "How lovely! You must know that the mountains are our ancestors?"

"Yeah," I said. I was familiar with the Māori concept but I hadn't really thought about it that much, even though Mum's mother's family is Māori.

"But down here, they won't be *our* ancestors. Our mountains are further north. Down here they will belong to the local iwi groups. You better find out who, so you can be respectful when you're visiting their ancestors..." Rosetta chatted away and I wondered what my class would think if I was suddenly doing rituals for some other people's ancestors... "And you've got to be careful up high, too," Rosetta continued. "The air is thinner up there – you're closer to being 'between the worlds' as they say."

I wondered whether I could talk to Rosetta about the Dreamrealm. Surely she would understand... but I didn't want to risk her telling Mum that I was having weird dreams again. I really did NOT want to go back to Dr Spancer or have to take pills. It was the pills that had made me an easy target for the Politician and Judgement. I shivered.

"What's wrong?" Rosetta said, picking up on my shift of mood.

"Nothing," I said. "Things have just been hard with all the changes."

"Oh yes," Rosetta said, carrying two mugs and a teapot over to the table where I was sitting. "Now, I brought this kawakawa tea from back home. I hope you like it."

Kawakawa... the same plant that had suddenly appeared

in the Grove a few weeks ago – that was probably some kind of message from the ancestors. Now's my chance to ask her...

And I did...

I only meant to tell her about the kawakawa bush but then to do that I had to talk about the Grove and about the dreams leading up to getting there, and about the whole Dreamrealm, and before I knew it I had spilled my guts and told her the whole story.

It felt so good to tell someone.

Rosetta was silent for a moment after I had stopped talking. It was so unusual for her to be quiet that I realised I had probably done the wrong thing. *I should have kept my mouth shut. She's going to tell Mum and we are going to have to go through all of that – all over again!* My chest began to tighten.

Rosetta looked at me, and suddenly she was beaming one of her big warm smiles and I knew everything would be fine. She understood.

I smiled back.

"You have the gift," Rosetta said.

"What?" I asked.

"Second sight," she replied.

"What's that?"

"You can see things other people do not – you can walk between the worlds." Rosetta sighed. "How wonderful!"

"I didn't know that was a thing," I said.

"Oh yes, my dear," she assured me. "It shows up in different ways – I have it too, you know, but for me it just means I see our tūpuna – our ancestors – sometimes. You know, my mother will pop in and give me a good telling off, or her father or my great grandmother will show up with a warning about something or another. It usually happens at night; I will see them at the end of my bed."

"That sounds creepy," I said. "Like ghosts."

"Oh, believe me, it would be creepy if I didn't know them, but you know, they are whānau, and family come and go as they please. You just have to get used to them putting their nose into your business."

I laughed, wondering if one day I would do that to my descendants, but then I guess I would have to have kids, which sounded kind of gross.

"Thanks for listening to me, Aunty," I said. "It's so good to finally be able to talk about all of this with someone. I can't talk to Mum because she just worries and tries to get me to go to a brain doctor."

"Oh! Your mother!" Rosetta said, raising her arms in the air. "Don't worry. I won't tell her a thing you've said, but it's just typical of her. She has the gift too, you know?"

"What?!" I could not imagine Mum talking to spirits or anything like that at all.

"Oh yes, she has never wanted to believe in it, so she always shut it out, but as a child, she would come to me and tell me stories and try to make it go away because she was so scared."

It was hard to imagine my mother being scared. I had seen her angry, but never afraid.

I sipped the kawakawa tea. It tasted a bit sour and made my tongue tingle.

"This is good," I said and gulped down more of the hot liquid.

"It's good for you," Rosetta replied. "Gets the blood pumping, helps with digestion… lots of other things."

"Why do you think the kawakawa plant appeared in the Grove?" I asked.

"That's a good question," Rosetta said, "It might be a message for you – that you need to reconnect with your ancestry, with your culture."

I didn't even know where to start.

"Come to think of it," Rosetta said, "I brought a gift for you that might be useful."

She reached into her handbag and rummaged around for a while.

"Here!" she said, triumphant, holding out her hand with what looked like a small dark stone in the middle. It was dull and vaguely egg-shaped.

"It's a… rock?" I said, a little disappointed that it wasn't something more interesting.

"Not just any rock," Rosetta said. She flipped it over in her palm to reveal the other side which had been cut, flat, and polished.

"Wow!" I said, looking into the dark mirror of the surface, it looked like tiny rainbows, shifting around as Rosetta moved the stone from side to side.

"What is it?" I asked.

"This is a seer's stone," Rosetta said. "I picked it up

at a little spirit fair on my way down. It wanted to come with me, and now I know why."

She picked up my hand and dropped the seer's stone into my palm, closing my fingers around it. She held my hand for a moment.

"This could help you – look into it and relax your mind – it's a bit like a crystal ball."

I laughed, imagining myself as a fortune teller covered in velvet.

"Seriously," Rosetta said, "you know more, deep down, than you realise, and this will help you to understand."

"Thank you!" I said, admiring the stone, turning it from side to side in my hand, appreciating the beautiful flecks of colour that changed as it moved. "What is it made out of."

"It's a stone called… let's see, I have it here somewhere."

Rosetta rummaged in her bag again and produced a small piece of white paper.

"Labradorite,"

"Like the dog?" I asked

"No, like the crystal, which in fact was named after a country – in fact I think the dog was too," Rosetta said, giggling.

She read the little piece of paper: "Supports strength and perseverance, balances and protects, raises consciousness and grounds spiritual energies. Excellent for strengthening intuition and promoting psychic abilities!"

I smiled as Rosetta read.

"See!" she said.

"It's beautiful!" I said. The crystal looked different from various angles, colours glinted through: blue, green, gold, purple, orange. They shimmered depending on how I held it. From some angles, the whole stone seemed to light up.

"How does it do that?

"Iridescence… it's nature's magic," said Rosetta. "But it's not just about how pretty it is. It's a tool, you know. It's called a seer's stone because you can look into it like… like reading tea leaves or something. You can look for signs, or clues, or messages."

"Do messages actually show up in it?"

"If you know how to read them," she said, staring at me with that look she often had – as if she was looking right through me to the other side.

"I don't…" I said, "I don't know anything."

"Don't be so sure," Rosetta said. "Just spend some time with it. Relax with it – you might be surprised."

"I can keep it?" I asked, excitedly.

"It's yours for as long as you need it," said Rosetta. "And eventually you may feel like giving it to someone else who needs it more; that's how it works with crystals."

"Thank you, Aunty Rosetta!" I hugged her.

"You're welcome, darling, but you might not want to make a big deal about it to your mum. She doesn't really appreciate things like that – and she might think I'm encouraging you in your dream fascination."

"What's that got to do with dreams?"

"Well, I think it might help you, in your dreams. Put it in your pocket when you go to sleep – see if it's still there in your dreams, or maybe just call for it while you are dreaming. I have a feeling that reading it will be different in dreams – clearer – maybe more magical."

As I held the stone in my hand I heard a cracking sound.

"What's that?" I asked, Rosetta. "Do you hear that?"

"I don't hear anything, darling," Rosetta said. "Just the birds outside and the sound of the fridge."

Suddenly my stomach felt like lead.

What's going on?!

CHAPTER NINE

That night, I went to bed with the seer's stone in my pyjama pocket, hoping that I could take it with me into the Dreamrealm. I was sure that if I could look at it there it would be even more amazing.

I had spent a lot of time looking at it since Rosetta gave it to me, but all I could see were the glints of changing colours. I didn't know how I could get any other meaning from it – at least in the waking world.

I relaxed into bed in my dark bedroom. I said the charm that Veila had given me, and found myself in the Grove again.

I looked down to see I was still wearing my pyjamas. I felt something hard in my pocket. I reached in and pulled out the seer's stone.

It still looked unremarkable from the back, a dark, egg-shaped rock, but then I turned it over. It gleamed under the swirling purple sky. The colours within looked more intense, deeper and more mysterious, with patterns shifting within.

I carried the stone along the forest path, into the meadow. I looked at its surface, it swirled around like something I'd seen before and images began to appear and fade. Mesmerised by it, I sat for a long time, watching, without thinking to ask anything in particular until a question popped into my head.

What do I need to know?

The image of a big old tree appeared in the stone, with a familiar outline. I recognised it as the Priestess Tree.

I wanted to check the dome, to see if it was actually cracking or if it was just my imagination, but I was feeling lonely, especially without Veila around. She was probably off doing her other work, whispering suggestions for dreams to other humans, to help them grow, streaming her words from a source even she didn't even understand.

Doesn't she see that I need her? I thought, as terror rose up. The meadow had darkened and the wind had picked up. There were none of the usual jellyfish in the sky, or anything else. It was just empty.

The Dreamrealm could sometimes be a frightening place when I was alone like this. I remembered I could fly, and pushed off from the ground as if in a big bounce, moved upward and glided towards the Priestess Tree. I could see it in the distance as I moved closer, but dark clouds swirled behind me in a menacing way. *Quickly,* I thought, *be at the tree – now.* I opened my eyes and swooped in to land at the foot of the Priestess Tree.

I could see the dome nearby, but it looked fine, with no visible cracks, at least from this distance. I didn't want to go any closer, at least not without Veila around.

I reached out to touch the tree. *I'm here,* I thought, *I need you... I'm worried that the fragments are escaping and I don't know how to find the Labyrinth and Veila says we are running out of time!*

Relax, said the familiar, calming voice inside my mind that I knew to be the tree.

All is well, she said.

I have a question for you, I said in my mind,

You want to know about the stone?

Yes.

And why it is similar to my vision mirror.

Yes.

And how to use it well.

What can you tell me? I asked

I can show you. I felt my mind being pulled down again, down, down, down into the earth to see the beautiful priestess's form, her eyes remained peacefully closed, the disc appeared in front of her belly – the same one she had shown me visions in before. I looked into the shimmering surface. In it I saw myself, holding my own, small seer's stone... only I looked different, my dark hair blew in the wind, curling around my face, my eyes shone, and I looked older, more grown up... wearing some kind of awesome dark purple superhero clothes including a big, gleaming, metal belt. I had seen something similar in Honu's mirror – the one I used to trap the fragments.

To work the stone, you must relax with it. Hold it, connect with it, relax... and then form a clear question in your mind.

Hold, connect, relax, form a clear question, I repeated in my mind, trying to remember it.

Yes. The more relaxed you are and the clearer your question, the easier the answer will come, and the better you will receive it.

Okay. Hold, connect, relax, form a clear question. I continued to repeat this in my mind.

Don't try too hard, the Priestess Tree continued. *Trying and pushing will cut you off from the source, from the flow, you must open up, you must relax in order for the messages to come through.*

I thanked the Priestess Tree and stepped back, excitement building in my chest.

And promptly woke up.

CHAPTER TEN

I just wanted to stay in bed the next morning. I was dreading going to school, but eventually, I reached over and checked my clock.

9:30!

I struggled out of bed, panic building in my chest.

Why didn't Mum wake me up?! Is she okay?

I heard the sound of plates clinking and voices in the kitchen.

It must be Saturday!

I sighed and rubbed my eyes, then I went out to see what was going on. Mum and Aunty Rosetta were sitting at the table, eating pancakes.

"Morning sleepyhead," Mum said, smiling at me.

I sat down and helped myself to pancakes with lemon and sugar, without saying a word. I felt mad at Mum for not waking me up earlier, but also kind of happy it was Saturday. I was aware that feeling mad didn't really make sense, and I didn't want to make a scene in front of Rosetta, so I just stayed quiet and gulped down a few delicious bites of breakfast.

"Awa," Rosetta said, she was wearing a long, flowing purple dress, and had violet-rimmed sunglasses propped on her head. "I have a special place to take you today. Please tell me that you're up for an adventure!"

"Of course!" I said, through my mouthful of food. All the weird feelings had disappeared in the excitement of whatever Rosetta was planning.

Mum drove us to Rosetta's friend's house, which was about twenty minutes out of town, in the countryside. She turned down a long, tree-lined driveway, and dropped us off outside an old brick house. It reminded me of my childhood home, the one that had been demolished just a few months ago... Even though that house had been made of wood, this place had a similar feel to it. I liked how there were lots of big trees, and that vines grew up the front of the house on one side.

Mum left with the car to go shopping, and Rosetta knocked on the front door.

"Gwyneth!" she exclaimed, as a white-haired woman opened the door. Rosetta introduced me to her friend and we went inside to have tea.

"Now for the real reason I brought you all the way out here," Rosetta said to me. "I know you are interested in labyrinths, and Gwyneth has one!"

I almost choked on my tea. "What?"

Gwyneth smiled. "It's nothing fancy," she said. "Most people think a labyrinth is a big maze, like in the film, but actually a labyrinth is not about tricks or dead ends. It has a single path..."

I looked at her, blankly.

"Most modern labyrinths are used as a kind of meditation," Gwyneth said. "They don't have high walls; they are paths in the ground that you can walk. Let me show you."

She stood up and we followed her out into the sprawling back garden. In between the trees, I could see a large circle of bricks laid in a winding symmetrical path.

"It's beautiful!" I said, as we walked over.

"You can walk it if you like," Gwyneth said.

I stepped self-consciously up to the opening in the path. Gwyneth and Rosetta must have sensed that I didn't want them to watch me, because they turned and walked away, discussing the roses.

I put one foot in front of the other, hoping that this waking-life labyrinth would give me some clue about the one in the Dreamrealm. As I walked I felt prickles on my spine as if I was being watched. I heard a strange, distant noise which sounded a bit like cracking glass. I felt a tightness in my chest and the familiar feelings of anxiety.

No... stay centred...

I focussed on just my breathing and on the path in front of me, following as it wound around and back again. I felt lighter somehow, as if this path of bricks was connecting me with something deeper, working its magic on me. I could see my anxiety for what it was:

just a pattern – just a bunch of thoughts and reactions... not something that had control over my life. The further I walked, the better I felt about myself, and my life. I emerged from the same entrance where I'd entered, feeling wonderful.

That night, in the Dreamrealm, Veila wasn't around *again*. I sat down on one of the boulders by the pool in the middle of the Grove. Cupping the seer's stone loosely with both hands, I relaxed my breathing and let myself stare gently at it.

I watched the patterns shimmer and swirl for a few minutes, then I allowed my mind to form a question – the one I had been wondering for a while now.

How can I get into the Labyrinth?

The patterns swirled into the shape of a bird – a sparrow, and then quickly changed into an apple, and then again, into the shape of a small stone.

What the hell does that mean? I wondered, but the patterns just reappeared in the same order: a sparrow, an apple and a stone.

"Hmm," I said to myself. "This is even more cryptic than the Priestess Tree!"

I went back out into the meadow and sat on a rock, which seemed just the right size for me. I could have sworn the rock wasn't there before. Like many things, it may have shifted in the Dreamrealm.

I held the stone in the palm of my hand and looked

into its shining flat surface. *What do I want to know?* I wondered. *I know, maybe I can use the stone to find Veila.*

I concentrated on Veila, on the way she looked, tiny and bright as if light shone out of her, always changing, always moving, never standing still for more than a moment. I remembered what the Priestess Tree had said about needing to relax. *Relax,* I told my body. I imagined the feelings of Veila – the feelings that I associated with her – of warmth and magic and kindness, and the unusual, exciting feeling I got every time Veila appeared in my dreams.

Veila... Where are you? The question formed clearly in my mind as I looked at the stone.

To my excitement, the surface of the stone flickered. Then, like a tiny projector screen, Veila was in the stone. I could see her, flying through what looked like tunnels. I didn't recognise the tunnels and I was disappointed. How could I get somewhere if I didn't know where it was?

Maybe I can, I thought. *It's my dream, after all.* I closed my eyes and focussed on the images in the stone, willing myself to be where Veila was. I imagined following the silvery thread of Veila's energy all the way to its source, flying there, wherever it was. I felt a breeze rush past me.

I opened my eyes and I was flying, fast, too fast. It was terrifying!

My gut felt like it jumped up into my throat. This was like a super-intense hydro-slide.

I was afraid I might die.

I tucked myself into the "turtle position" that we had to do for earthquake drills at school, and landed, with a thud, in my bedroom.

Except it wasn't my bedroom. The walls were pink, edged with daisies and there was a poster on the wall of Cheriez, a pretty pop star that I hated because her music got stuck in my head whenever I heard it on online videos.

"Awa?" Veila said.

"It worked!"

"Shhh!" Veila responded. "She's sleeping?"

I looked over towards the bed and recognised Felicity's face, asleep on the pillow.

"She's… I know her!" I whispered. "She's really mean."

"She seems pretty harmless to me," Veila said, then she looked at me, "– but – wait – how did you get here?"

I explained about the stone.

"This is quite remarkable," Veila said. I flushed with pride at her words, maybe I was getting the hang of these Dreamweaver powers after all.

"I've never heard of such a thing!" Veila continued. "You've entered into the liminal waking world through your dream! I mean – really, you shouldn't be here."

"What do you mean, liminal?"

"Well – I can't, myself, enter the waking world properly as I'm a creature of dreamscapes, but I enter into the in-betweens. That's what liminal means. So here, no one is awake. This child is sleeping peacefully, and I can come and do my work – whispering to her the suggestions for dreams that will help her to grow into deeper awareness."

"I'm awake," I pointed out.

"No – you're a dream creature like me – look, you have no legs again."

I looked down and gasped. "You're right."

"You really shouldn't be here!" Veila said, "I have a number of protections over me in order to do this work but you are not safe – we can't risk that you get stuck here, outside your body."

"That sounds awful! How do I get back?"

"Try going the way you came – and please – don't try to visit me when I'm working – I will find you when I have time."

I felt guilty all of a sudden. I hadn't thought this through. I hadn't thought about whether Veila would want to see me. I hadn't thought about whether it would be safe and now the terror crept higher and higher – what if I was already stuck here?

Relax, I recalled the voice of the Priestess Tree.

I closed my eyes and willed myself back to the meadow, imagining a thread back to the feeling of being there. I waited until I felt the flying sensation before opening my eyes again. It did look like I was moving through tunnels. But the tunnels were made of strands of light, all woven together into streams that I could dip my hand into. The sensations were similar to a stream of water, but somehow more energising. It made my spine tingle.

I landed in the meadow.

A sound broke through the usual calm – that same cracking sound I had heard while I was awake.

What the hell is that?

I looked down into my hand at the seer's stone. *Maybe I can find out.*

I relaxed my mind again and gazed at the swirling patterns on the stone. *Tell me,* I thought, *show me what that is... what is going on?*

A shape appeared in the stone. It looked like a ball. *What does that mean?* I wondered. At first, I thought of a tennis ball, or a basketball, even a crystal ball, but then as I moved the stone gently from side to side I noticed that around the ball were trees and hills.

It isn't a ball at all! I realised. *It's a dome!* It was clearly the dome by the Priestess Tree – the one I had trapped the fragments in. As I looked at the image in the stone, cracks started to appear at the top of the dome and run down the sides.

I knew it! That's where the cracking is coming from!

"Veila!" I called out. I knew that she was busy and that she did not want to be disturbed – but this was clearly more important!

I began running towards the Priestess Tree, calling out to Veila again and again as I ran. I had to see if it was true.

This is the last thing I need, I thought. *Things are hard enough in my life without the Dreamrealm being under attack too!*

I could see the dome in the distance. It looked calm and peaceful, sitting there – too calm and peaceful.

I could not see any cracks running down the sides, like the stone showed. The dome looked the same as it had for weeks – large and foggy.

"What is it?!" Veila appeared with a small popping sound next to me. "I *told* you I was busy and then you keep calling me anyway!"

"Veila!" I said. "Veila, the dome!" I pointed up to it.

"What about it?" She asked.

"It – I saw it in the seer's stone – it's cracking… I keep hearing these cracking noises in my waking life and just now I heard the same thing here."

"What?" Veila said. "It looks fine."

"Maybe we just can't see the cracks," I suggested. I had circled around the base of the dome by then and Veila was right, there were no visible cracks.

"Maybe they are at the top?" I suggested.

"Let's have a look," Veila said, fluttering upwards.

I bent down and leapt up to follow her, rising higher and higher like a helium balloon.

We hovered over the top of the dome. I squinted into the light reflecting off the glass. Sure enough, there were cracks – tiny hairline fractures, just at the top of the dome.

"Can we do anything about them?" I asked.

"You can try," Veila said. "But it might be a trap."

I remembered how the fragments kept trying to trap me last time.

ISA PEARL RITCHIE

"I wouldn't touch it, if I were you," Veila said. We floated back down to the ground.

"I have to do something though," I said.

"Maybe just… visualise it. Imagine the cracks closing up again." Veila suggested. "You stay here and I will go up and check to see if it's working."

I looked at the dome, trying to capture the image in my mind before closing my eyes. I relaxed my mind again, remembering how I'd made the dome trap the fragments, just a few weeks ago. Imagined energy flowing up through the ground, rushing over the dome, harnessing the warmth of the sun, flowing into the cracks and setting them like glue.

"It's working!" Veila called out. "Keep going!"

I did keep going, until every single tiny fracture in the glass was filled, bringing the dome back to its former strength. Then I imagined another layer: a golden coating of protection covering over the dome, just to be sure we would be safe.

I opened my eyes to see Veila floating down again with a big smile on her face.

"Nice work!" she said. "See, when you focus you can do great things with those Dreamweaver powers!"

Something was still bothering me.

"Veila, if it happened once, surely it will happen again – the cracks, I mean."

"Surely," Veila repeated. "Yes – but hopefully by then you will have mastered the powers of alchemy."

I sighed. "I haven't even found the door to the Labyrinth."

"All in good time," Veila said.

I looked up at the Priestess Tree and across the meadow, only to hear the familiar sound of my mother calling me.

"Time for school, honey!"

"No!" I tried to call back the meadow. "I'm not ready."

But I was in bed, with legs and everything.

"What's that you've got there?" my mother asked from the bedroom door. I looked down, only to find the seer's stone in my hand. *How strange... it was in my pocket when I went to sleep!*

"Nothing," I told Mum. "Just a stone I found."

"Why were you holding it in your sleep?"

"I don't know!" I yelled, suddenly grumpy. "Leave me alone, I need to get dressed!"

I got dressed fast and packed my bag for school. I rushed out the door before realising I had forgotten the seer's stone. I went back for it, but I couldn't see it anywhere in my bedroom.

It's gone!

I had been so distracted with worries about losing the seer's stone and the dome cracking that I had almost forgotten about the school camp – until it was only a day away!

It was a last-minute rush to pack everything I needed from the list Mr Jasper had given us, plus a quick trip to the shops with mum, later that night, to pick up a torch and gumboots.

"It's lucky that shops are open late these days," Mum said, "but I wish you told me earlier."

"You're the mother here," I said. "Shouldn't you be reminding me of this stuff?"

Mum just sighed. I knew what she was thinking: I'm old enough to be more responsible, blah, blah, blah...

Dad called me that night and said he hoped I had a good time at camp – and then he reminded me that he was about to go away overseas on a business trip for a whole month!

"But I haven't seen you in ages!"

"I know, honey," Dad said, "and I was really hoping to see you before you left – but work has just been so..."

"Busy," I said. "Yeah, I know."

"But you're going to be away at camp, anyway, Awa," Dad said. "And I'll be back before you know it."

My heart sank. I was missing Dad already. Camp was only for a few days, and I knew it would be a long month.

There was still no sign of the seer's stone and suspicion flared in my mind.

"Where is it?" I asked Mum. "The special stone I had – that you saw me holding, in my room. I can't find it and I know you took it."

"Don't be so rude, Awa," Mum replied.

"It was important!" I yelled as I stormed to my

bedroom. "Aunty Rosetta gave it to me. You had no right to steal it. Give it back!"

"I haven't taken anything from your room," Mum called out. "But I'm sure it can't have disappeared. Why don't you clean your room?"

I slammed my door and slumped across my bed, my eyes darted around the room in search of the stone, but it wasn't there. I looked across at the piles of books and clothes. It was probably messy for other people, but I knew if I cleaned my room I wouldn't be able to find anything. There was no seer's stone in sight.

If Mum didn't take it, where could it possibly have gone?

I had to get up early the next morning to get to school on time, and for some reason, I didn't have any dreams that night. I didn't think very much about it at the time. It would have worried me more if I hadn't been in such a rush.

It was still dark when we got to school. I packed my suitcase into the luggage bay, and climbed on the bus, waving goodbye to Mum.

Ella and Evan were already squashed into the back of the bus and so I took the nearest available seat next to some kid I didn't really know and who slept most of the way.

The sun had properly risen by the time we pulled into the dusty campground.

"Okay, everyone over here!" Mr Jasper called out. "I'm going to sort you into your cabins."

He began calling out names. I was gutted when he called Ella into a different cabin list and even more devastated when he called out my name: right next to Felicity's! I was going to have to share a cabin with her and her annoying friends.

Felicity had barely spoken to me. She had actually been pretty quiet since the incident a few months before, when she had to apologise in front of the whole school. The only time she'd spoken to me since was when she'd said she wished I never existed, which was actually pretty mild by her track record. I knew deep down she was still a bully and I did NOT want to share a cabin with her.

CHAPTER ELEVEN

J went and got my bags and chatted with Ella for a while. She commiserated with me over being in Felicity's cabin.

"You should see if you can swap into our cabin," Ella said. "After what Felicity did to you it's really rude that they would put you two together."

I sighed. "You heard what Mr J said – no swapping, this is the final list."

I carried my bags to the cabin.

Felicity was already in there with her friends. They were gathered around the bottom bunk on the far side of the room.

I put my bags next to the empty bunk right by the door, just to be as far away as possible.

"Ooh! I love this eyeshadow!" one of the blonde girls said. I glanced over and saw they were looking at a big pile of makeup in the middle of the bed. "Where did you get it from, Felicity?"

"My dad gave it to me for Christmas," Felicity replied. "It was super expensive, he got it in on his way back from a work trip in America."

I sighed, *am I going to have to put up with this for the whole camp?*

"Do you know what this one is?" I heard Felicity say. I looked over to see she was holding up a small sparkly pink tube.

"Oh my God!"

The girls shrieked and gasped.

"You've got it!"

"Is that the Valerie Sparkles gloss?" one of them asked. I glanced up again.

"My mum would never let me buy it – it's so expensive," said the first blonde girl again. "You're so lucky!"

I felt my stomach tighten, remembering my conversations with Mum that had gone the same way. I stole another quick glance across at the tube Felicity was still holding up. She moved it from side to side so the girls could watch it shimmer.

I didn't *want* to want it. It wasn't even purple – it was pink! But something in my gut just wanted to reach out and take it. *Is this jealousy?* I wondered. It was different from how I'd felt before when I had seen other people with things that I wanted. This was way more intense. *It's just a stupid lip gloss,* I tried to tell myself, but I still couldn't stop thinking about it.

We ate our packed lunches out under the trees. I sat with Ella, and Evan, but my mind kept flipping between worries about the dome cracking in the

Dreamrealm and wondering how long my fix would hold, resentment that I had to share a cabin with Felicity, away from my friend, and horrible jealousy that Felicity had that lip gloss and I didn't!

I couldn't believe the teachers had put me in the same cabin as Felicity. After everything that she'd done. They were probably just trying to force us to get along. I briefly considered telling mum about it, but Mr Jasper had confiscated all our phones, and I didn't want to worry her or seem like a cry baby.

"Now, we have a surprise for you," Mr Jasper said, raising his voice to talk to us as we ate.

Whatever the surprise was, I had a feeling I was going to hate it.

"In about twenty minutes we are going to go across to the huge obstacle course on the other side of the campgrounds," Mr Jasper announced.

Great... just great I thought, *the last thing I want to do is embarrass myself in front of all these kids with my lack of sports skills and coordination.*

CHAPTER TWELVE

*T*he obstacle course didn't seem *that bad.* Mr Jasper led us out to what looked like a huge wooden playground – although instead of the bright colours usually associated with a playground, this was all natural wood with a bit of dark green and brown thrown in for good measure – which made it look like a park for army soldiers.

The other kids seemed more excited than me, but at least I wasn't freaking out. We began climbing up the ladders and across the bridges, balancing on the planks of wood as we made our way through the obstacle course.

I looked across to the other side, where some very determined kids had already gotten to. There was a kind of tower, made out of wood, and I saw that we had to go up there and then climb down a huge rope. My stomach tightened, imagining all the ways I could embarrass myself on that thing.

I watched the other kids. It looked like they were having fun. Maybe it wouldn't be so bad.

By the time I got across I was feeling more confident – I hadn't even fallen off anything so far, so maybe this would be alright too.

It was my turn to take the rope. I reached out – I couldn't quite get my hand around it – it was too wide – so I did my best to grab hold with both hands and wrapped my legs around underneath me. I just kind of hung there on the rope, for a while, feeling it burn the palms of my hands. I tried placing one hand under the other but they started to burn so much that I couldn't hold on.

I loosened my grip and let myself slide down a bit instead, but that fiery burning increased as the rope slipped through my hands. *Ouch!* It was too late. I had let go and I was falling. I grabbed hold of the rope with one hand; it yanked my arm up, just as my left foot hit the ground on a strange angle.

Pain jolted up my leg and down my arm. I collapsed onto the ground.

"Awa!" the kids around were calling, "is she alright?"

I heard the voices but I didn't really know who they belonged to.

I felt dizzy.

I saw Mr Jasper's blurry outline as he approached.

"Are you alright, Awa?" Mr Jasper asked.

"Yeah," I said, pushing myself up – as soon as I tried to stand the pain jolted back up through my leg. "I… I don't think I can walk," I said.

I looked down at my feet – they looked normal, in my slightly dirty sneakers, but my left ankle was like jelly when I tried to stand on it –

"Ouch!"

Very *painful* jelly!

"Okay – let's get you back to the campsite and see what we can do," Mr Jasper said. Turning to the rest of the kids he added, "We're going to have to cut this short. Back to camp everyone!"

There were sounds of frustration and disappointment from the kids who'd been enjoying the obstacle course. I felt even worse… and it didn't make things any better that Mr Jasper had to hold my arm to help me limp back to camp – *so embarrassing!*

Ella ran over and held me up by my other shoulder, making it somehow less embarrassing because I wasn't just walking with Mr Jasper anymore. She talked non-stop about her aunt's pet dog, Scrunchie. I think she was trying to distract me from the pain; it wasn't working, but it was better than her just worrying about me or asking me how I was feeling, which I guess most people would do.

"Didn't you hurt your foot just a few weeks ago?" Ella asked.

It was true – I had fallen in the Dreamrealm and woken up with a sore foot. It had shown me that getting hurt in my dreams carried through to the waking world; anything dangerous that happened in the Dreamrealm could risk my life for real.

"Maybe I just have weak ankles," I said to Ella. It

wasn't a very good explanation but she seemed to accept it.

They half-carried me to the sickbay at the camp. One of the parent helpers, who was a nurse, looked at my ankle.

"It looks twisted," he said.

"Twisted?" I asked.

"Sprained," he explained.

Of course, I had heard of that before but I thought it was just a little thing – not something that could cause so much intense pain.

"I can't even walk," I said. I was sure it must be broken.

"It's a bad sprain," the nurse guy explained. "Let's put some ice on it, and see how it feels tomorrow. A bad sprain like this should be fine in a few days."

Days? I thought, *camp only lasts a few days. Maybe I can use this as an excuse to go home and get away from Felicity!*

Mr Jasper was not convinced. I tried to tell him that really, my parents would prefer me to be home and that it was the responsible thing to do, but he said I had to stay and participate as much as I could.

I sighed.

It's going to be a long week!

CHAPTER THIRTEEN

he nurse helped me to limp back to the cabin to rest. As we made our way slowly through the camp, I heard the tittering sound of laughter and glanced around to see Felicity and some of her friends huddled together, looking at me.

"Faker," Felicity whispered, just loud enough for me to hear. The word struck me as strange. *Why would I fake something like this? How could I, when it's obviously an injury?* I felt my face flush with anger. *Why does she have to be so mean?* But the pain in my foot distracted me from any further thoughts. We turned the corner to face the cabins.

"This one," I said, pointing out the room I had to share with Felicity and her friends.

I plonked down on the bed and closed my eyes. *Maybe I can dream.* But the sun outside and the noise from the other kids were too distracting. I dozed for a while, then sat up and looked around.

Felicity's makeup lay on her bed, just across the room. I looked over at the shining pots, tubes and bottles. I had never been into make-up, but the lip gloss was the one by Valerie Sparkles and Mum had absolutely refused to get it at that "outrageous price!"

I got up and limped over to look more closely. It was not the shade I would have chosen. Felicity had gone for a pastel pink, whereas I would have gone for a purple. I picked it up. As I held it, the tube sparkled like the stars in the galaxy in my dream... as if it were meant to be mine.

I could just take it.

I heard a noise. Quickly, before thinking twice, I pocketed the lip gloss and was back in bed, with my eyes closed. I heard the other girls come in and I ignored their sniggering.

My heart still racing, I rolled over, touching the smooth tube in my pocket, feeling the exhilaration of having done something I shouldn't have.

At dinner time Ella came and found me and helped me limp over to the dining hall. We were having Bolognese which was not half as nice as the one Mum made, and there was no hot sauce in sight – we weren't allowed to bring our own condiments, believe me, I had checked. I ate in silence, trying to force down as much as possible because I knew eating would help me sleep better.

"This is good," Ella said "– but you must think it's so bland, Awa."

It was nice to have a friend who knew me well

enough to understand, but even that thought made me feel anxious that I might lose her friendship, that she might realise what a freak I am, that she might choose Evan over me… I pushed the anxiety away and reached into my pocket, feeling the smooth tip of the lip gloss tube. My anxiety was replaced by a rush of excitement from knowing what I'd done.

"Yeah, pretty much," I said. "I wish I had just smuggled in a little bottle of hot sauce – this could really do with more flavour!"

The thrill of taking the lip gloss faded into a gnawing guilt in the night. I tossed and turned. I couldn't sleep, even though I was missing my dreams, and I was terrified that something bad might be happening in the Dreamrealm. Every time I moved, my ankle ached, and the guilt from stealing the lip gloss made me feel sick. *What have I done?* I wondered, *and why did I do it?* I didn't even like pink. I didn't really need lip gloss. I thought about putting it back in the morning but I felt the clinging urge to keep it. There was a greater burden too: *what if I get caught?*

"Do you need some help, Awa?" Anna, one of the other girls in the cabin asked.

They were getting ready for the morning assembly in the hall. I had been wondering how I would get over there when my foot was so sore.

"I might," I admitted. I had managed to get up and get dressed in my bed, but my foot still hurt too much to stand on it properly.

"I can help you walk over there when you're ready," Anna said. She sounded much nicer than Felicity's friends usually did, although I didn't I knew I had to be careful not to let her see the lip gloss. I had to hide it somewhere. Something told me not to leave it in the cabin. I checked to see no one was looking and quickly stowed the lip gloss deep into the pocket of my shorts. I put some other things on top to make it less obvious.

Anna held my arm and helped me limp over to the hall for morning assembly, followed by a breakfast of corn flakes and rice bubbles. The other kids went mountain-biking that day. I was allowed to stay back at the hall and draw, which suited me; I wasn't too sure of my mountain biking abilities, even without my ankle sprain, and I was scared of falling off the bike!

I drew pictures of Dreamrealm, of the purple swirling sky, of Veila and the Priestess Tree. The coloured pencils the teachers had given me were not able to capture the vividness of my dreams, but maybe nothing could accurately reflect them. After a while it was quite lonely, sitting there.

The other kids returned before lunch, but I stayed in the hall, drawing, while they played around outside. I was so focused on what I was drawing that I didn't notice Felicity approach.

"Hey Awa," Felicity said.

I jumped. "Hi."

"Have you seen my lip gloss?"

"Your what?"

"My lip gloss, the one I had yesterday – the one from Valerie Sparkles."

My heart raced and blood rushed to my face.

"I have no idea what you're talking about," I lied.

"I bet it was you," Felicity said. "I bet you took it – and by the way, the sky isn't purple!"

Felicity turned and stormed out of the hall, leaving me with both relief and my guilt.

Is it the guilt that is stopping me from getting into the Dreamrealm, or is it something to do with the fragments?

I tried to reassure myself that it was all probably just a coincidence as I walked back to the cabin, with Ms Phillips' help. As we arrived, straight away I noticed my things were not how I'd left them.

"You might want to keep your stuff tidier, Awa," the teacher said.

"I didn't…"

All of my things were out of my bag and strewn over the bed.

Ms Phillips had already left before I could explain, which was probably a good thing. I didn't want her to be suspicious about why anyone would go through my stuff.

Felicity, I thought. *She must have been looking for the lip gloss.* I was relieved that it had been in the bottom of my pocket all along, though now it felt like such a burden to keep it there, such a risk. I checked to see that no one was looking and took the lip gloss to Felicity's bunk, carefully slipping it down the side of the bed. Then I returned to my own side and began packing up my things.

CHAPTER FOURTEEN

The other kids were playing ballgames in the hall, but I couldn't join in even if I wanted to because of my ankle, so I sat, bored, under the fluorescent yellow lights, watching. After a while, I yawned and realised I was quite tired.

"Can I go to bed?" I asked Mr Jasper.

"Sure, have a good sleep."

I limped out of the hall, relieved to get away from the noise.

It was dark outside, with no moon in the sky. I had no shoes on because my swollen ankle made me unable to fit in my sneakers. I felt the soft grass under my feet. As I slowly moved closer to the cabins and further and further from the light, my toes struck the gravel of the road that went right around the campsite.

"Ouch!"

No one could hear me this far from the noisy hall.

I tried to limp over the rough stones with their

sharp edges, but it would have been painful enough with two good feet. I was unable to put much weight on my sore ankle. The pain of the gravel was unbearable. I tried again, and again. I even knelt down and tried to crawl. The sharp stones cut into the soft skin around my knees and tears swelled in my eyes. I looked back towards the hall but it was too far to limp all the way back; my ankle felt sorer than ever. I sat back on the grass and collapsed in sobs.

I looked around at the darkness.

Something could be out there, watching me...

Would I be stuck here for hours? Would everyone forget about me? My heart started to pound in my chest. Would I be taken by kidnappers? All my fears burst up. Fears for my own life and for my family. *What if Mum is hit by a car while I'm away at camp and I don't even know? What if Mum and Dad are both killed and I have nowhere to go? What if I die here, alone in the dark? What if a murderer comes?*

I shook myself.

Stop. This isn't helping.

I took a deep breath. *I'm afraid and that's okay; that's normal. It's just like Veila said, I need to accept my fears so I can move on.*

I relaxed a little into slower breathing. Then I heard it: the sound of footsteps on the gravel, moving closer. My mind darted back to kidnappers and murderers. I was helpless. There was no way to escape.

"Hello! What are you doing there?"

The woman's voice in the dark was familiar, but could not place it.

"I have a twisted ankle and I can't get back to my bunk… I can't walk over the gravel," I told her, "It's too sore on my foot."

"Here, let me help you," the woman's said. She helped me up, then she swooped down, picked me up, and carried me over the gravel, and towards the cabins. I was impressed by how strong she was – to be able to carry me so easily.

As we neared the light on the other side of the cabins, I looked at the woman's face and gasped. It was so like Felicity's in the low light.

"Are you okay, dear?" Felicity's mum asked.

"I'm okay. Thanks," I said.

"Which cabin are you?"

"This one," I gestured.

Felicity's mum opened the door and walked in, "And which bunk?"

"The bottom bunk on the right."

I felt myself being deposited, safely into the softness of my own sleeping bag, and fell quickly into another dreamless sleep.

CHAPTER FIFTEEN

$\mathcal{I}$ was feeling dazed the next day at camp. Things seemed to go past in a blur. Suddenly all of the other kids had gone off and I was left by myself, with just a few parent helpers who were busy doing chores around the campground. I decided to go for a walk to the river, since I'd missed out when my ankle had been much worse the day before.

I remembered what I had been told – to follow the path straight ahead until I reached an orange safety cone which marked a large muddy puddle, then to turn off. I couldn't quite remember the direction though. The kids who had been there the day before, when I was resting my ankle, had brought rose petals, picked sneakily from the roses outside the camp office, and had sprinkled them along the path to show each other the way.

"Follow the rose petals," Anna had said, when I mentioned I might go to the creek while the others were out doing much more active things. I couldn't see any rose petals yet. I walked through the pine needled path, looking at the rows of pine trees on each side.

I felt good, beneath the trees. It reminded me of the Dreamrealm forest path, of walking along between the meadow and the Grove. I was happy I'd waited and come down here alone. It was much more peaceful without the other kids who might tease me for limping a little bit.

My foot still hurt, but only slightly, now.

As I cleared the pine trees I saw the orange cone up ahead. It was sitting in a puddle. I looked around. Two big paths ran, to the left and right, but I still could not see any petals. I took another step towards the cone and sighed. Maybe I could just choose a path and wander until I found the creek, or turn back and try the other way.

As I started to turn I noticed something I hadn't seen before – a third path, narrow and winding, through the grass that snaked around behind the cone. This path felt more likely. *But how did I only just see it now?* I wondered. It had seemed invisible just moments before. *And where are these rose petals?* I still couldn't see them, but as I moved closer to the path something pink gleamed that I had not noticed before – a petal, and another one, and quickly I saw that they were scattered right up to the big path I was standing on, only a few feet away. They were there, all along, just like the little path.

I began walking the path through the grass, towards the stream.

I could hear the sound of running water up ahead. The trees thinned then opened up to the wide blue sky. The stream was several meters wide but not very deep. I took off my shoes and dipped my feet into the water. It felt lovely and cool.

I couldn't really swim in here; it was too shallow, and I wasn't allowed to swim without adult supervision anyway. I sat down on the bank in the long grass, enjoying the refreshing feeling. It had been a tough few days. I hadn't participated in many of the camp activities, some of which I was glad to miss, but others seemed like fun.

What's the point of being here if I can hardly do anything with this ankle?

I could walk on it now; it was much better than the previous two days, but the kids were tramping in the bush today and that would have been too much for my foot to take.

I didn't mind being alone, it was just that sometimes loneliness crept up on me... the feeling of emptiness.

I closed my eyes to try to keep that feeling away, listening to the birdsong and the rushing of the stream, feeling the cool water. Veila, *can you hear me?* I wondered if it was possible – *maybe if I relax enough, I could have a waking dream.*

I listened, but there was no response.

I opened my eyes and looked around again. Things

seemed brighter, it was a bit like the path being revealed, maybe I could see more now.

I heard a whisper at the back of my mind, like Veila's voice but more in the way that the Priestess Tree spoke – an internal whisper:

Choose four stones.

I looked down at the stones below my feet. They glistened in various shades, the way that stones do underwater.

Choose one for inspiration.

I reached into the cool water; my eyes locked on a stone with a reddish hue. I plucked it from the stream and examined it: the deep colour that I knew would fade as it dried, the black veins stretching across the deep terracotta surface.

Choose one for wit.

I reached out for a light, specked stone, then listened again for the voice

Choose one for health.

I skimmed my hand over the pebbles in the bottom of the stream, before it settled on a slightly larger, darker stone with small cream and brown flecks and spots.

Choose one for the heart.

I reached for a stone that gleamed green in the underwater light. It seemed to shine, almost as if it was calling to me. It had lighter veins thought it, like marble, and deeper green patches.

These are your touchstones, Veila's voice seemed to whisper.

"What do I do with them?" I said aloud, "What are they for?"

Hold them when you need guidance, hold them when you need rest, hold them when you need healing, hold them when you need insight...

The voice was interrupted by a sound.

"Awa!"

Someone was calling my name. One of the teachers must have come looking for me. I quickly slipped the stones into my pocket and put my shoes on. I walked back in the direction of the camp, through the pine trees.

The stones jangled loudly in my pocket.

A warning; the words flashed in the back of my mind.

But a warning about what?

I looked around but I couldn't see where the voice had come from. There were no people in sight, just the feeling that I was being watched. I started walking more quickly, checking behind me and through the trees for threats, looking for movement. I heard a thud on the ground. *Probably just a pine cone,* my logical mind told me, but everything else inside screamed: *RUN.*

I ran, as fast as I could with my ankle still sore, hoping I didn't make it worse. The stones clacked together in my pocket as I sprinted along the pathway through the trees and out into the safety of the open field, where I paused to catch my breath.

Why is it that the field feels so safe when the forest doesn't? I wondered.

There are fewer unknowns, Veila's voice sounded in the back of my mind, and I was grateful not to feel alone.

Am I safe here? I asked Veila.

Keep moving, Veila replied. *You're safe for now, but keep going just in case.*

Just in case of what? I wondered as I walked back towards the cabins, but there was no reply, and I had a feeling I didn't really want to know.

CHAPTER SIXTEEN

I lay in bed that night in my bunk and remembered to say Veila's charm. I followed the patterns behind my eyes into my dreams and into the Grove. I noticed them straight away, lying on one of the boulders: the four stones I had chosen from the river.

They gleamed in the soft light of the clearing, sparkling much more than they did in waking life, especially after they had dried.

"Veila?" I called.

Veila appeared in the Grove, hovering in mid-air above the pond at its centre, her internal light shedding reflections onto the water's surface.

"That was the first time you've come straight after I called you," I said, surprised.

"I can't always come."

"Of course, you have better things to do with your

time than hang out with me," I said, feeling a bit sulky. It had been a hard day.

"Not better, just different," Veila said, ignoring my complaints. "What do we have here?" Veila continued.

"These are the stones – you helped me choose them at the river?"

"Did I?"

"Yes – I was awake and I called for you and heard your voice."

"Oh, so I did – I thought I imagined that," Veila said.

"Don't you think everything is imaginary anyway?"

"So I do," Veila said, fluttering over the stones. "Pretty."

"They are, aren't they?" I said.

"What are they for again?" Veila asked.

"That is exactly why I called you!" I said, "I thought you would know what to do with them!"

"I know what to do with them," Veila said. "I just didn't see which one you picked for which thing. Which one is for inspiration?"

I didn't know how, but I still remembered each stone, as if I'd always known their meanings.

"This one," I said, holding up the stone with the reddish tone.

"Okay, so this is the stone relating to Fire," said Veila. "Sit down somewhere comfortable, hold it and then just relax, okay?"

I sat on one of the boulders. I closed my eyes, and relaxed, holding the stone between my palms. Nothing –

for a moment – and then, as if a flint had lit a spark igniting something inside, I felt a rush of energy, coming so fast I barely had time to understand one thought before it had been replaced by another, and then another.

"Wow." It was exhilarating, but there was no chance I could remember any of these ideas, let alone write them down.

"It's too much," I said. "I can't make sense of it."

"Just relax. See what lesson the fire stone wants to teach you."

I relaxed into the rush of energy. The pace seemed too slow. *What is my lesson?* I asked in my mind.

A whispering voice replied: *all of this is within you, we do not contain inspiration, we just give you a glimpse of your own potential.* I took a moment to take this in; all the brilliant rushing ideas were really my own. *You can find inspiration when it feels like you've run out of ideas,* the stone continued, *and we can help you focus.*

I opened my eyes.

"Wow," I said, still buzzing with the feeling of rushing inspiration. "Hey, why does the stone refer to itself as 'we'?"

Veila looked at me sideways. "Clearly, you have not done much talking to stones before, have you?"

"Of course I haven't," I said.

"Stones are not individualistic," said Veila. "They don't think of themselves as 'I' because they still feel connected to all the other parts of their original form, even when separated for thousands of years."

"But I just pulled random stones out of a river – why is it that this one has a lesson about inspiration?"

"Nothing is random, and everything is," Veila said.

"That doesn't make sense."

"It's synchronicity. Stones have many lessons, and the one you chose when I called for you to find one for inspiration is the one that came to you for that lesson. That is just how it works."

"Shall I try another one?" I asked Veila.

"Sure," Veila replied, "…but let me try something first. Lie down this time."

I replaced the red stone and picked up the green one that Veila gestured to. It felt cool in the palm of my hand.

I lay down on the soft grass of the clearing.

"Okay – so this is the stone of the element of water. Hold the stone close to your heart. I'm going to put something over your eyes," Veila said.

She darted away and returned with a big leaf.

"Close your eyes," Veila said.

I felt the cool sensation of the leaf over my eyelids. Swirling colours swam around inside my head.

"Now, just relax," Veila said in a calm, soothing voice. "Relax and listen to the stone."

I felt a gentle rushing this time, like water flowing towards me, pooling around me. It felt wonderful. I relaxed as the water carried me in its gentle stream, connected to all the other streams, the oceans, connected to the entire world.

"It feels good… so connected."

"It is a universal truth," Veila said, "that we are all connected to everything, all the time."

"It feels like everything is made of pure joy."

"Clearly," Veila replied.

I sat up and pulled the leaf away from my eyes. "But if that's true, then why is there all this suffering?"

"That's another question, altogether, and another story."

"But it doesn't make sense!"

"That is part of it," Veila said.

I took some time holding the other two stones. The earth stone was the dark stone I'd chosen for "health." It felt as if it connected me with the earth itself. I felt heavy and solid when I concentrated on it. The stone I had chosen for "wit" turned out to be for the element of air, and it felt light and full of potential.

"But – what – what is all this?" I asked Veila. "What are these stones for, anyway?"

"They are tools that you will need."

"I just found them in a river, how can I need them? And what will I even need them for?" I asked, frustrated.

I wanted to go back to the stream, where everything felt good, but it seemed like a lie compared to all the struggles in life.

"You will need them to face the Shadow," Veila said.

A chill ran down my spine.

"The Shadow, like you've talked about before?"

"The very same."

"Why do I need to face the Shadow?"

"This is part of why you are here, in the Dream-realm... why we are all here. We are working towards the expansion of consciousness, Awa – that means we have to face the Shadow, even though it's terrifying. It's not just you, or me. It's also about all of humanity and the things you humans do not want to face."

"What?" I said, "like atrocities and war and murder and... climate change?"

"Exactly," said Veila. "Everything that is too hard to deal with, that is suppressed, or buried or denied... all of that becomes the Shadow."

In my mind, the Shadow appeared now as a seething mess of disgusting and awful things... that somehow I had the responsibility to face. I shuddered.

"What if I don't want to?" I asked.

"That is understandable," Veila said. "But we must all play our part, and your courage will grow."

"I'm not scared!"

A cracking sound broke through the dream, waking me up, but when I looked around, safe in my camp bed, all I could hear were normal morning sounds.

Oh no... I thought. *I need to do something before it's too late!*

CHAPTER SEVENTEEN

The next day was kind of boring, but at least my ankle was feeling better. The other kids teased me, especially Felicity. They kept saying I was just faking to get out of camp activities.

To make things worse, I hardly saw Ella or Evan at all. They seemed to be spending a lot of time together and not making much effort to hang out with me – just like I had feared.

I went to bed on the final night of camp, exhausted. I tucked the river stones under my pillow. They looked dusty now, and grey, compared to how they had gleamed underwater and in the Grove. I was only halfway through Veila's charm when I arrived in the Grove.

It always surprised me that no matter how tired I was in my waking life, I usually arrived in the Dream-realm feeling refreshed and energised. It was true this time too, despite my worries about the dome cracking and the fragments escaping.

Maybe it's something to do with this place, I thought, looking around at the beautiful stream, the tall trees, the wildflowers and berries. The river stones sat on the big boulder by the pool, where I had left them. They glistened in the soft light of the Grove.

Veila popped into view, right in front of me, startling me.

"There you are!" she said, as though she had been waiting a long time. "I've been looking all over for you!"

"Hi," I said. "Are you going to make me practise using my powers again?"

"Of course," said Veila.

"Veila, I don't even know what I'm doing."

"Not with that attitude!" Veila said. "You better figure it out fast, you know we are running out of time."

"Look, I know we are," I said. "I'm scared about the cracking sound – I'm scared the dome will crack open at any moment and we will all be in danger again!"

I rested my head in my hands. *I need to know more... the Priestess Tree and the gulls haven't helped much... Maybe Honu can help me.*

"Let's go!" I said to Veila, who just looked at me, curiously. "Let's go and ask Honu."

I put the stones into the front pocket of my pyjamas. They fit in the dream even though I didn't think they would have in waking life.

I walked out of the Grove to the meadow, Veila following close behind. As I walked, I wondered if I could somehow teleport myself over to the lake to see Honu – like the time I was being chased by the Politician and Judgement, when I suddenly popped back into the Grove.

As I walked, I closed my eyes and concentrated. *Nothing.* I still felt the path beneath my feet, the forest all around. I tried again, this time imagining the lake, the grainy texture of the sand under my feet – I could almost feel it. I heard gulls calling in the distance and opened my eyes to see that I was there!

I looked out across the gorgeous, shining purple surface of the lake. I could see Honu nearby, partially submerged in the water so that he looked just like an island.

"Honu!" I called out.

The giant turtle moved closer to me, raising his head from the water, sending waves rippling all around.

"Greetings, Dreamweaver," he said in his deep, resonant voice.

"I need to ask you about these," I said, holding the river stones.

"I see you have found your touchstones," Honu said.

"Actually, they were just some rocks I picked up at a river on my school camp," I said. "I'm not sure why they are so important."

"It is not the stones, as material objects of earth and mineral, that are important," Honu said. "It's their meaning for you – it is how they help you to connect to the elements we are made of: earth, air, fire and water. The Dreamweaver must understand with the grounded solidity of earth, the intuitive feeling of water, the mental clarity of air, and the passion and energy of fire. It is only through connecting with yourself through these elements of being, that you may master your powers and alchemise the fragments."

"Honu, I'm just guessing here, but do I need to take these stones into the Labyrinth?"

"That is an excellent guess, Dreamweaver," Honu said, not entirely answering my question.

"Okay, but I can't even find the doorway!" I said.

"Ho ho ho," the turtle laughed, the deep vibration of it sending ripples across the surface of the lake. "You have found the doorway," he said. "You have been there before."

"How do you know?" I said, feeling confused.

"I have my ways of seeing," Honu replied. "And since you seem to need a bit of help, you might consider going back to the Priestess Tree."

"She just shows me images I don't understand!" I said in exasperation. "I need to figure this out now, Honu. We don't have much time before the fragments figure out how to get free and come after us again!"

"It will all become clear," Honu said, "and much sooner than you think. You keep looking outside for answers when they all lie within you. I am certain that you already have all the information you need."

I heard a tiny jingle of bells as Veila popped into view next to me.

"There you *are*!" she said. "You were right there and then you weren't... I've been looking everywhere for you."

"Sorry," I said. "I didn't mean to freak you out, I just somehow managed to teleport myself over here."

Veila looked at me blankly.

"I was walking along the path," I continued, "and then I really concentrated on being here, and suddenly I was."

"That's brilliant!" Veila said, doing backflips in the air. "You'll be mastering your Dreamweaver powers in no time."

"Honu said I need to take the stones to the Priestess Tree," I told Veila. "And maybe on the way we can check to see if there is more cracking in the dome."

"Can you Telly-pour again?" Veila asked me.

"Hah! I can try," I said. "But don't look at me, it feels awkward."

"I'll meet you there!" Veila called and disappeared.

"Farewell, Dreamweaver," Honu said. "And remember – let the stones be your guides."

I watched him sink back down into the lake.

Okay, I thought, *time to 'telly-pour'.* I giggled.

I relaxed and focussed on the Priestess Tree, willing myself there, concentrating as hard as I could.

I felt the change, the grass beneath my toes, the light breeze on my skin. I opened my eyes to see I was back in the meadow. The dome stood to my left and the Priestess Tree was to my right.

Veila hovered next to the dome.

"There is no cracking," she said, "I checked."

"I *know* I heard cracking," I replied.

"It must be a trick," Veila said, "to try to get you to do something that will free them."

I shivered.

"Let's go," I said, leading Veila towards the Tree.

As I approached, I could see something was different. The bark of the tree had changed.

"Did someone come here and hurt her?" I asked Veila, my pulse quickening. "Look at her bark!"

"I don't think so," Veila said, in a far more relaxed tone than me. "Take a closer look, what do you think?"

I saw that there were four holes in the bark, making a kind of diamond shape between them.

"What…" I started to ask as I moved closer, then I felt the stones clink in my pocket. *Four holes, four stones… it can't be…*

I turned to Veila, "Do you think she's expecting me – and the stones?" I asked, "Do you think she wants me to put them into these holes?"

"That's exactly what I think," Veila said.

I looked slightly closer and noticed the small hollows in the bark were slightly different colours, with patterns inside. I gasped, "They match the stones!"

Veila just giggled, finding my surprise hilarious.

I matched each stone to the colour of the hollow and put them in.

Now what? I asked, holding my palm up to the Priestess Tree to see what she had to say.

Take a step back, and watch, came her reply.

I took a hasty step back, not sure what was going to happen.

I watched as the stones began to glow and smoulder in the hollows, their outer layers peeling back to reveal gemstones beneath.

Wow.

I waited until the stones stopped smouldering before I approached the Tree again. I held my palm back up to speak to her.

Take these stones now, close to your heart, and let them guide you to the Labyrinth.

I took the stones from the tree hollows and watched as the bark in the tree wrapped itself back up to look as it usually did. I saw the image in my mind again that the seer's stone had shown me – a bird, a stone, an apple.

The images faded away and I was left staring at the stones. They glimmered in the palm of my hands – it was strange to think these had just been ordinary river stones... and they probably still would be in the waking world.

The red one had become vibrant – the colour of raspberries. The light speckled one was now yellow; the green one was now the green-blue of the earth's oceans and the brown one was a deep earthy colour that shimmered in the light.

Close to your heart... The Priestess Tree had said. I

looked down and saw my front pocket hanging open. It was exactly where I had put the stones before and it was kind of over my heart. I gently tucked the stones back in there, feeling them clink lightly against each other.

"Now what?" I wondered out loud.

"What did she say?" Veila asked, gesturing to the Tree.

"She said they would guide me... but how?"

Something flashed in my mind.

"I've got an idea," I said to Veila, "but I might need you to keep watch and make sure I'm safe."

"What's your big idea?" she asked.

"I'm going to fly up – as high as I can, over the Dreamrealm, and then I'm going to close my eyes and see where the stones guide me."

"That does sound dangerous," Veila said. "You're right – I better keep watch and tell you if you are about to crash into anything or..."

Neither of us wanted to think about the other dangers, of the freaky fragments lurking in the dome, or the creepy and mysterious Shadow, or the possibility of being attacked again. I hoped Veila was right about the dome, and that the fragments were still trapped inside where they could not hurt us.

I crouched down, in preparation for the big jump I needed in order to fly. I sprang up, rising higher and higher. The Priestess Tree and the dome looked like children's toys below me. I could see the forest spreading out to the side of the meadow. As I rose higher I caught a glimpse of the lake where we had just been, and the snowy mountains in the distance, and the stretch of desert below them. On the other side, the soft green hills rolled out towards the sea. I kept rising higher until I could see the entire Island of the Dream-realm spread out below me.

I was up so high that my spine tingled.

"Veila!" I called, and watched as she floated up next to me.

"Are you ready?" she asked.

I wasn't sure I would ever be ready – but I nodded anyway.

Closing my eyes was terrifying, and I was a bit worried I would wake in a falling-dream and lose all the progress we had made.

"Okay," Veila said. "What now?"

"Let's just go down gently, slowly," I said, "and see where we land. Hopefully, the stones will guide us."

I could sense the stones in my pocket. I imagined them guiding us to the place we needed to find: the entrance to the Labyrinth.

"Uhhh... okay," Veila said, "but you are going to have to relax."

I knew she was right, but it was terrifying, being up there, above everything, exposed.

"This," Veila continued, "is a bit like what you needed to do to get into the Dreamrealm in the first place – out of the Rooms of Mind – do you remember?"

I thought back to that early waking dream. I played

on a rope swing over a ravine. I had to fall, to let go, to trust.

I nodded.

I slowed my breathing. I wasn't thinking about anything in particular, but I felt the wind whip past me and realised I had started to move.

It's working!

There was a falling sensation – the bottom of my stomach felt like it had just dropped, but still, I kept my eyes closed and counted my breaths.

"You're doing great!" Veila said, "and don't worry, there is nothing in your way."

I kept my mind as blank as possible. When thoughts came up I let them go and just focused on my breathing, on relaxing, on the feeling of the air as it moved around me.

Something gently touched the tips of my toes. I felt the tingle of Veila holding my hand as we came to land on soft, damp grass.

I opened my eyes to see that we stood directly in front of the Elisiad Tree.

"This can't be right," I said. "It's just a tree."

"Just a tree!" Veila said, laughing at me. "You humans really are strange. Of course it's a tree... but so much more. Anyway, we're here now. There must be a reason."

"The gulls told me to re-trace my steps!" I said. "This must be what they meant. I came here – it was the way you showed me to get back to the Dream-realm." I turned and looked in the direction of the seacliffs. *The entrance is in plain sight... that's what they told me... I could see this tree from the Elisiad Tree... I have to find the entrance.*

I approached the tree, looking around for some kind of entrance. I couldn't see anything.

I tried placing my hand against the trunk, but nothing happened.

"What did Honu say?" Veila asked me.

"He said I had all the information I needed."

I sighed.

That doesn't seem true at all...

I walked around the tree again, looking for clues, but found nothing.

"Do you remember last time you came here?" Veila asked.

"How could I forget?" I said. "The fruit from the Elisiad tree is the best thing I ever tasted... do you think I could have some more?"

"Awa, pay attention," Veila said. "What else do you remember?"

"I sort of... just sat here for a while. I think I had to relax and pay attention to my breathing or something... you called it centring."

Veila nodded.

"Okay... so I'll try that again."

I tucked the stone into my pocket and sat, cross-legged, at the base of the tree and closed my eyes.

I focussed on my breathing, centring my energy inside myself, letting go of all my other thoughts.

After a while, I felt something drop into my palms. I

opened my eyes, hoping for more Elisiad fruit, and gasped.

Instead of fruit, the thing in my palms was much more precious.

It's the seer's stone!

"Look!" I said to Veila, holding the stone up so that it shone in the light.

"Amazing!" Veila said. "You did well."

"But how did it come back?" I asked. "And how can I find it in my waking life?"

Veila just shrugged. "You're the one who did it. Hey, look!"

I turned to see that the ground around us had morphed and shifted. Something bright and round had appeared at the base of the tree. On closer inspection we found it was a golden tunnel, gleaming in the sunlight.

"How strange!" I said. "Should we go in?"

"After you," Veila replied.

I stepped carefully into the tunnel.

"Eeep!" I cried. My feet slipped and my heart leapt in my chest as I began to slide. I held tight to the Seer's stone in one hand, with my other hand holding down my pocket, as I continued slipping down the enormous shining slide, deeper and deeper under the Dreamrealm.

After what felt like miles of sliding, I landed with a thud in a deep dark cave. Veila was close behind me.

"What should we do now?" I asked.

"What do you think?" Veila replied. "You're the Dreamweaver."

In the darkness, I could see something glowing at the edge of my vision.

The river stones!

I took the stones out of my pocket, putting the seer's stone in there instead, to keep it safe. The colourful stones seemed to glow brighter in my hands, pulling us left.

I looked at the dark path in front of us. A tingle of fear prickled my spine as we walked into deeper and deeper darkness.

The dark was so thick it made the light from Veila and the stones seem dimmer.

That doesn't make sense, I reminded myself. *They should seem brighter in contrast to how dark it is.*

"What's that?" Veila asked.

I could hear a rumbling sound.

Panic rose in my chest.

A landslide?

Would we be trapped in here forever – or at least until we were crushed or we starved to death? Is it even possible to starve to death in your dreams? I wondered, remembering how hurting my foot in my dreams had carried through to the waking world, and realising it was the same foot I hurt at camp too.

I thought of how little I had eaten here and realised I probably didn't need to eat to survive. This calmed my worries a bit, but I didn't want to dream in darkness for the rest of my life and I didn't know if my teleportation could work in here. *It's worth a shot*, I thought.

"Veila – we have to get out of here – I'm going to try teleporting," I said.

"What are you talking about?" Veila asked, confused. "You can't teleport in here… in fact, I'd be surprised if you could use any Dreamweaver powers with the air so thick and dark, and so far from our realm."

"But it's dangerous! We need to escape."

"Awa – I thought you wanted to find the entrance to the Labyrinth."

"I do – but not if we are going to be crushed by rocks!"

"Awa?"

"What?"

"Look!" Veila gestured to the wall in front of us.

Dust and stones were falling away revealing something underneath.

"It's a door!" I said, all thoughts of escaping disappeared just as the rumbling sound came to a stop.

"So this is the entrance," I said, walking towards it. "I wonder if I can just…" I tried to push the door.

Nothing.

I heaved with all of my weight.

"Veila, help me!" I said, "Help me get it open!"

Veila laughed.

"What?" I said, giving up and turning back to her. "What's so funny?"

"It's clearly not that sort of door," Veila said.

"What?"

Veila just looked at me.

"You're not being very helpful," I said.

"I don't have much power, down here," Veila said. "This is too far from my realm."

"Well, that's just great," I said sarcastically, looking out into the dusty darkness all around us. "What am I supposed to do now?"

"Honu told you that you already have all that you need."

"All I have is some rocks."

I tried holding the river stones up to the door, but nothing happened.

I wish the stones would just open the door – like a key... but they didn't seem to do anything useful.

I looked at the stones in my hand. They glowed softly in the deep darkness. I could see the lump in my pocket.

That's right... the seer's stone.

Somehow, I had forgotten about it. I took it out of my pocket with my free hand and looked at its shimmering surface.

Show me...

I relaxed my mind, like the Priestess Tree had told me, and gazed into the seer's stone, which began to swirl. It was only slightly illuminated by the glow of the river stones, and somehow that made the images that appeared even clearer.

A sparrow, an apple on a tree, a stone...

"Not this again!" I said, explaining the images to Veila.

The stone door began to shake. The surface cracked slightly and dust cascaded from it, onto the ground. Then everything was still. I tried again to push the door open, feeling that its surface had become rougher, but it remained in place.

"What was that about?" I asked.

"Look at it!" said Veila, "look more closely – what do you see?"

I turned back, holding the stones up to the door. In their light, I could see tiny markings on the door – engravings. They looked like they might tell a story but I had no idea what they said.

"So what do I do?" I asked, frustrated.

"We need to figure it out," Veila said.

"You make it sound like it needs some kind of code," I said.

"It's something like that,"

I took a closer look at the markings. There was something that could have been a bird, and the shape next to it look a bit like an apple, and then there was an imperfect circle... *a stone*.

"That's what the seer's stone showed me!" I said. "Maybe it's some kind of code – like, we just need to decipher it – to say them in the right order of something."

"You could try," Veila said, looking sceptical.

"Bird! Apple! Stone!" I heard a distant rumbling, but nothing else seemed to change.

I tried again.

"Apple, bird, circle."

Nothing.

I kept trying, using as many variations I could think of. Nothing seemed to work. Eventually, I gave up.

"I finally got this far and now we're stuck," I said.

I sank down to the ground, resting my back against the side of the cave, my head on my knees, feeling hopeless.

I can't believe I've come this far and now I'm stuck.

"What are you doing?" Veila asked.

"I'm..." I started, then I kind of saw myself, "I guess I'm doing what my mum would call 'sulking'," I said.

"What for?" Veila asked.

"It just seems too hard."

"Rock is hard," Veila said. It usually frustrated me when she said such silly things but I didn't have the energy for frustration.

"Whatever," I said.

"No," Veila continued, "I mean, it's hard, down here, under the rock. I told you. I don't have much power here."

I looked up at Veila, noticing her light looked much dimmer than usual.

"I can't stay down here for much longer," she added.

"Maybe we should just go," I said. "It's not like we're getting anywhere."

"It bothers me how easily you give up," Veila said, "and how much you push for things to happen before they are ready to – you know, when the fruit is ripe..."

Something clicked in the back of my mind. *Fruit... apple...*

"Wait – that song!"

"What song?" Veila asked.

"That song you usually sing – tell me all the words to it... you know, it goes 'when the fruit is ripe...'" I couldn't remember the rest of the words.

Veila began to sing.

> When the fruit is ripe, it will fall,
> Not through any effort at all
> By being ready to let go.
> At the right time, it knows!

I repeated the song after her and heard a rumbling behind the door. "It's working! I said – is there any more?"

"Any more, what?" Veila asked. Her eyes were closed. Her light was fading.

"Song!" I asked. "Does it talk about a bird?"

"What, how did you know?" Veila asked.

"I think it's what these images on the door are about – the bird, the rock and the apple," I said. "They are the same things the Priestess Tree has been trying to show me for ages but I didn't know what they meant."

"Are you serious?" Veila asked.

"What? Why?" I asked.

"It's from an old Dreamrealm proverb – 'Befriend the sparrows we cannot chase and pluck the apple when is if ripe, just as the seed must be left to sprout alone.'"

The door rumbled even more and then stopped.

Is that all?

I tried singing it again but there was no more movement. I slumped over, feeling defeated, but as I sat there in the dark, something whispered to me from the back of my mind.

Maybe it doesn't just need the words; maybe it needs the understanding.

"What does it mean... the proverb... the song?" I asked.

Veila came to rest beside me, deep in thought, after a while she began to speak. "Some things that you want in life are like plucking an apple from a tree – you just reach up and take it... but..."

"But only when it's right," I said. "Yeah I get that part, patience, blah blah blah..."

"Do you really get it?" Veila asked. "You don't sound patient."

I sighed. "I'm trying. What about the sparrow?"

The door continued to rumble. I wondered whether it would move enough that the stones above would fall and we'd be trapped here.

We've got this far... we have to try.

"Other things are more like a sparrow," Veila continued, after a pause.

"Sure they are," I said. "Sparrows are kind of a pest."

"Not like that," Veila said, sternly. "Have you ever tried to pick up a sparrow?"

"That would be impossible," I said, "...unless it was wounded or something."

I felt like I was on the edge of understanding the proverb, and every time I figured out more, the door started rumbling again.

"These are the things we can't easily control – unlike plucking the apple, where you can just reach out for one," Veila said.

"– or get a ladder for the higher branches," I suggested. "But yeah, I get it. You have to wait until the fruit is ripe. There's no point in trying to force something that isn't ready... so it's like these are different types of things – different metaphors for achieving outcomes."

Veila nodded.

The door continued rumbling.

"A sparrow will hop away if you chase it – if you make any sudden movements," I said, still feeling confused, but the door continued to rumble beside us, so I figured I was still on the right track.

"So what do you do?" Veila asked me.

"Please tell me you don't hit the sparrow with the rock," I said. "Like killing one bird with one stone."

"What?!" Veila asked.

"It's a waking-life proverb," I explained, "except it's two birds with one stone..."

"What an awful thing to say," Veila said, shaking her head. "No. Tell me how you would make friends with a sparrow, instead."

"Uhh... I could lure it in somehow... leave it food...

but that's not enough," I said, remembering an online video I watched, where a monk was friends with sparrows. He said he was just still, and they came to him. "I have to be still," I said, "allow it to spend enough time with me to know it's safe."

"Yes," Veila said. "This is what many things are like – you can't simply pluck them from the tree. You have to build trust with life."

Veila's words hit me in the face.

"I don't trust life," I said. "Why should I? I never know what's going to happen next, I just know that bad things happen…"

But life brought me here… to this point…. the little voice in the back of my head whispered and something clicked.

"Exactly…"

The rumbling behind the stone door became so loud I could hardly hear Veila.

"So what about the stone?" I asked, raising my voice above the sound of moving earth.

"That is the easiest of them all," Veila said, "the stone just is…"

"You don't have to befriend it, you don't have to wait for it to grow, you can just pick it up!" I said, remembering the stones in my hand. I held them up towards the door again like an offering.

Dust fell from the walls around the door as it began to visibly swing open.

Finally!

I looked at Veila. "Let's go," I said.

She shook her head.

"I can't go in there," she said, "It's too deep underground. You will have to go alone."

"What? No!" I said. Behind the door was absolute darkness. The thought of going down there alone, into the dark, was terrifying enough to make me want to wake up.

"You've come this far, Awa, and this is as far as I can guide you."

"Guide me?" I said. "You've barely done anything, and now you're just going to leave me here – alone?"

"I do have some advice for you."

"*Really*?" I asked, still mad.

"Keep to the right side as you enter. Run your hand along the side of the cave – walk right up against the walls." Veila said. "It's what the last Dreamweaver did... It will help you to avoid holes in the middle of the path, or other obstacles. The Labyrinth has many twists and turns. You do not want to lose your way. You might never get out!"

"Right... anything else?" I asked, through the sinking dread. I knew there was no point in arguing anymore – I really had to do this.

"Yes – trust your intuition. It will guide you. If you meet anyone in there, don't be scared, just stand strong in yourself. They can't hurt you if you are centred."

A tingle ran down my spine at the thought of meeting anyone – anything – in that dark tunnel.

Stay focused, I told myself. *Don't let the anxiety thoughts start. Don't get freaked out. Stay centred.*

"You need to place the four stones at the four corners of the Labyrinth," Veila said. Seeing the look of confusion on my face, she added, "the stones will help to guide you when you get close."

I looked down at the stones, still in my hands, their glow was too faint to light up the dark tunnel. I put them in my pocket, ready to step into darkness.

"Oh wait – I forgot something!" Veila said.

I turned back towards her as she passed a small bag towards me.

"Here," she said.

"What?"

"In here are some berries from the Grove," Veila said. "I picked them earlier thinking they might help you – you know, to restore your energy while you're down there in the dark."

"Thank you," I said to Veila, smiling. *How can I be mad at her now?* I thought. *That's such a sweet thing to do.*

I took the bag of berries and stepped into the dark.

CHAPTER EIGHTEEN

I walked deeper and deeper into the Labyrinth. The stones clinked occasionally in my pockets as I went. I ran my hand along the side of the cave, terrified that I might get distracted and lose all sense of direction. I walked carefully, grateful that it was flat so far – without so much as a pebble to trip over – but every step into complete darkness was a terrifying unknown.

After a while, I wondered where I was going, and how far I still had to go. I felt tired and bleak. I just wanted to give up but I knew I couldn't do that. I had come this far and I needed to carry on, no matter what.

I remembered the little bag Veila had given me. I reached inside and picked up a berry. I had no idea what it looked like in the dark. I just put it into my mouth and let the juice trickle out of it. *Delicious... refreshing... calming.* Veila was right – it was the perfect thing to give me for my journey into the Labyrinth.

I continued on into the silent darkness. *I'm under-neath some part of the Dreamrealm,* I thought, *maybe the meadow... but am I still in the Dreamrealm down here... or is it someplace else – some different realm altogether? Veila can't come down here after all.*

A sound interrupted my thoughts. I stopped, standing absolutely quiet.

Something is there, I thought, *and I don't want to know what it is.*

The stones in my pocket seemed to be glowing brighter. I covered them with my hands, trying to block out the light, wanting to be invisible to whoever was out there.

Everything was silent. After a while, I figured they must have gone so I kept moving.

"No, no, no, no!" I heard an unfamiliar high-pitched voice echoing from the dusty darkness.

I froze.

"No… this is all wrong."

I stepped forward, curious to see who it was and what was wrong.

A tall, skinny figure stood in front of me, with hands over their eyes. They didn't seem to be dangerous.

"Ummm, hello?" I said.

They jumped, then said, "Who… who said that?"

They were visibly shaking as they peeked out at me through their fingers.

"Are you okay?" I asked.

"Of course not! It's you, isn't it?"

"Umm..."

"Everything is wrong," they continued.

"Can I help?" I asked

"No, no, no... you're part of the problem."

"Uhh, okay," I said. I didn't want to waste any time, and apparently there was nothing I could do to help the worried creature. I was guessing it was some kind of fragment because it seemed quite stuck.

"Well, I think I better get going then," I said.

"No, no... it's terrible in there," the worried fragment said. "You'd better come with me."

"I don't think so," I said, and took a step forward.

The fragment jumped out of the way as though they were terrified that I might hurt them.

"No, no, no!"

I continued to hear the voice, getting quieter as I walked deeper into the Labyrinth.

After a while, everything was quiet... *too quiet.*

A shriek sounded up ahead of me.

I froze again.

"Who approaches?" asked a voice.

I didn't know what to do. This was either the time to be brave or run away, and neither seemed like a very good idea.

"Reveal yourself!" the voice continued.

A light appeared up ahead. I braced myself and walked slowly towards it, noticing a bright yellow glow was now shining like a lamp from my pocket. I reached in and pulled out the yellow stone. It looked so different now; I could hardly remember which one of the river stones it had been, let alone what it was for.

I held it up, remembering that Veila said it would guide me, hoping that it would also protect me. As I walked towards the light my jaw dropped.

In front of me stood a rock, and on that rock rested a large and majestic bird.

"Who are you?" the bird said, as I approached.

"I'm Awa," I replied, feeling less afraid now.

"What is Awa?"

"I'm… I'm a Dreamweaver… apparently."

I saw the bird's eyes widen. I'm not sure how I knew, but something told me he was male.

"I have been waiting for you, Dreamweaver," he said. "I am Kahu, the hawk of dawn, and I see that you are bearing the stone that belongs in the east."

He nodded to the stone in my hand.

"East?" I asked. I had no sense of direction under-ground – not that I could normally tell which way was east.

"Yes, the direction of east – the element of Air."

"That sounds right," I said, remembering that the stone in my hand had once been the light specked stone of air.

I looked at the large hawk in front of me. "Why are you here?" I asked, not meaning to sound rude.

The bird drew himself up to his full height and puffed out his chest. "I am the guardian of the east," he said.

"Do you live underground?" I asked.

"Of course not," the bird chuckled, "I merely come here when I am called to guard."

I shrugged. "Okay," I said. "So what do I do with the stone."

"You don't want to keep it for yourself?" the bird asked. It felt like he was testing me.

"Why would I want to do that?" I wondered. I was getting a bit sick of carrying these stones around and this whole process of learning how to be a Dreamweaver was already taking me too long.

"To harness its powers of course – great powers of wit and cleverness. You could be the best and brightest. It could all be yours."

I wondered what it would be like if I somehow became really good at maths – the smartest kid in class. Everything would be so much easier, but I had a sinking feeling in my chest, like sea-sickness. The image of the hoarder came to mind – that creature who wanted to take everything for itself to the point where it spent its whole life carrying around a big pile of rags and jewels. I thought back to the lip balm and felt guilty. I had already taken something that wasn't mine, and I wasn't about to do it again.

"No," I said. "I'm here to put it in the Labyrinth – where does it go?"

Kahu let out a celebratory caw. "Excellent!" he said, hopping off the boulder.

"Put it here, on the direction stone of east." He leaned his head back towards the boulder where he'd just been standing.

As I walked towards the boulder the stone glowed brighter and brighter. I noticed that the light surrounding Kahu had come from the boulder itself, which also seemed to glow brighter as I got closer.

I placed the stone down and the light expanded so that all I could see was brilliant yellow-white.

"Time to wake up!"

No, I thought, *I need to know what happens next*.

"Wake up now!"

I could hear the teachers calling us to pack up camp. I rolled over in my bunkbed. At least I would be getting out of here!

CHAPTER NINETEEN

*P*acking up camp was so exhausting that I wished I could go back to sleep. I didn't really want to be back in that dark labyrinth, but I did want to see Kahu again. I knew I needed more information and I had to find the other direction stones... they were somehow connected to mastering my Dreamweaver powers, even though I didn't really understand how it all worked.

Once I had my bag packed, I double-checked to make sure nothing had been forgotten. I looked under the bunk beds and felt around the crevice between the mattress and the base.

My fingers grazed against something cold and hard. I reached deeper, wrapping my hand over the rounded object and pulled out...

The seer's stone!

My eyes widened in shock.

How could it be here when I lost it back at home, before camp?

I tried, but I couldn't find a logical explanation... *it must be more Dreamrealm magic.*

I was so relieved to have it back. I tucked it safely into my pocket, feeling the river stones clack together in the pocket on the other side of my jeans.

Felicity had glared at me while we packed up and I was glad to get a seat as far away from her as possible on the bus – at the back with my friends.

"I wish we could stay at camp forever," Evan said.

I was glad he had a good time; at least *someone* did, but I couldn't wait to get out of there.

As the bus drove along the dusty roads, I thought back to my dream again, and the things Kahu had told me. There was something familiar about what he said... *guardian of the east... the air... east and air.*

I had heard something like that before... somewhere. I pulled out my phone and looked it up.

A bright-coloured website came up about the four elements: air, fire, water, earth... *Just like the four river stones,* I thought. They each had different meanings and related to one of the four directions. The east was air, and the west was water, but the other two were different depending on what hemisphere people are in. In the Southern Hemisphere where we were, the south was earth and the north was fire. In the Northern Hemisphere it was the other way around. *I wonder if this is what's going on in the Labyrinth,* I thought. *Do I place each stone in the direction it belongs in? Which hemi-sphere is the Dreamrealm in?*

We arrived back at school after the long drive. A group of parents were waiting by the gate, ready to collect their kids. Mum wasn't there, and by the time she did show up, most of the other kids had gone and I was feeling grumpy.

I was silent on the drive home. Mum tried to talk to me – to ask me about camp – but I didn't want to talk about it. It felt like my tiredness, and all the stress of the camp, hurting my ankle, the loneliness, having to share a cabin with Felicity, and the guilt about the lip gloss – everything – was swirling around inside me. It was a bit like anxiety, but also like motion-sickness, and I didn't know how to deal with any of it.

"Don't forget to unpack your bag, honey, before your room turns into a pigsty."

"You're always trying to control me!" I yelled.

Mum looked shocked at my words, and part of me found that kind of satisfying – because it was one tiny thing that I had power over in my life when everything else was a horrible mess.

"Excuse me, Awa. You've only been back from camp for five minutes and here you are, attacking me!" Mum said.

I slammed the door.

Mum always wanted me to tidy my room and get rid of things I didn't need anymore, *why does she have to keep telling me what to do with my life?*

I looked around my bedroom. It did seem small and

cramped with all the toys and books I could not bear to throw out.

I don't need any of this stuff, I realised. *I'll show her, I'll throw it all out and see how she likes that.*

I grabbed a pile of boxes from beside the hallway door, left-over from the move. I began shoving things into them without thinking – everything I came across, almost everything I owned. My touchstones from the river were still in my shorts pocket. They clinked against my leg occasionally.

I filled the boxes, one by one, taking them out to the lounge and placing them right in the centre of the floor.

"Oh, Awa!" Mum said. "You're not – you're not throwing out the doll's house that Koro made for you? And these books – they're special. Some of these were mine when I was a kid. You'll regret not having them one day."

"*You* keep them then," I said, rage still burning in my chest.

"Why are you so angry at me?"

I looked at my mother, her shiny dark hair that always looked so neat, her face that everyone reminded me looked like mine. Her shoulders slumped and I felt a bit sorry for her.

I sighed. "I'm not, I'm just angry," I replied. "Okay, I'm a little bit angry with you, but I'm just angry with life in general."

I went back to my bare room. Tears came, thick and fast, flowing down my cheeks; I didn't even know why

I was crying. I lay on the bed, clutching the touch-stones, wishing everything about my waking life was different as I drifted off to sleep.

The room was dark, with just a crack of light under the door. I opened it to see the lounge bathed in grey light. The boxes I had packed were floating, suspended in mid-air. I walked around them, watching them as they stayed perfectly still. *Obviously, I'm dreaming,* I thought, *but how did I end up here.* I realised I was too tired and angry to eat dinner or to say the enchantment that would get me back to the Grove.

"Veila!" I called out, afraid of the creepy grey scene in front of me. I wanted to get back to the meadow, to lie on the soft grass and look at the purply sky, but I had no idea how to get there from here. *I must be inside the Rooms of the Mind,* I realised, *I don't like this place.*

I didn't want to start exploring; I didn't know what was behind the doors and didn't want to find out. I crouched into a ball and tried to imagine my way out.

"Veila!" I called again. There was no answer.

It's my dream, I reasoned, *so I have the power to find a way out of here – I bet I could fly right through this ceiling if I wanted to and up over the Dreamrealm to any place I like.*

"Awa?" I heard Veila's voice and looked around to find her emerging from the doorway. "Why aren't you in the Labyrinth? Where are we?"

"Oh, no… I woke up and then I fell asleep without saying the charm. Maybe I'll have to start all over again." I sighed. *Will I ever get through the Labyrinth?*

"This is…" I looked around to make sure. "This is

my lounge at home, but obviously I'm dreaming – so I think we are in the Rooms of Mind."

"It's strange," Veila said, "…I didn't know they did that in your world."

She gestured to the floating boxes.

"They don't."

"What are they?"

"They are the boxes I packed yesterday or today, I'm not sure… I packed up all my childhood toys and books and I'm going to throw them out because I'm not a baby anymore."

"You seem sad about it."

"I'm not!" I said, but I could tell she had a point.

"…and angry," Veila added.

"I… I don't know why," I admitted, "I'm just so sick of everything. I feel so powerless in my life. I just want to change things, but I can't!" I sobbed, a single tear emerged from my left eye and began to float in mid-air, swelling to the size of my head.

"I don't think I've ever cried in a dream before," I said. I prodded the tear with my finger and it burst like a bubble, saturating the room. "Gross!"

"Why is it gross?" Veila asked, wiping her tiny face.

"Now everything is covered in my tears."

"Are they bad?" Veila asked.

"I don't know – they're just – they come from me so they feel too… close."

"Is that how you feel about your childhood things too?" Veila said, approaching a box and popping her head in to take a look. She pulled out my favourite childhood toy, my bunny Bobo.

"I guess so – hey, what are you doing?"

Veila had started dancing around the room with Bobo.

"Waltzing!" she responded. "Is this how you do it?"

"I don't think so," I said. "When they do it on TV it looks quite different – you're just flying around with Bobo, holding his arm out in one direction."

"Bobo?"

"He was my toy rabbit from when I was a baby."

"And you want to throw him out?"

"I don't play with him anymore."

"Is that why you're so sad and angry?"

"I was feeling like this before I started sorting out my room."

"Feelings do that, don't they?"

"Do what?"

"They're like magnets," said Veila. "You know, you feel happy and smile and other people around you smile and you feel happier."

"I don't know, I don't usually feel like that," I said.

"Or you feel sad," Veila continued, "and then you do things that make you feel sadder."

"I guess so," I said. "Can we… can we just get out of here?"

"We could – but you are the one keeping us here," Veila said.

"I am not!"

"Yes – your feelings – they are pulling you here like

a magnet, or pulling this," she gestured around the room, "to you."

"So what am I supposed to do?"

"Just relax – try repeating the charm I gave you to get to the Grove – if that's where you want to be."

I lay on the floor of that strange room and closed my eyes…

CHAPTER TWENTY

I finished the charm, but something was different. I could tell before I even opened my eyes that I was not in the Grove. Darkness surrounded me. There was no difference whether my eyes were closed or open. The ground was hard beneath my feet. I reached out to feel the rough wall of the Labyrinth.

I can't get back to the Grove using the charm... What if I'm stuck in here?

As my eyes adjusted to the darkness I looked around. I recognised the outline of the hawk, Kahu, against the faint yellow glow of the river stone.

"You have returned, Dreamweaver," Kahu said.

I nodded.

"Tell me, where do you go when you are not in this realm?"

"The waking world," I said.

I tried to tell Kahu about school, about the apartment, about my parents and my friends. He listened, but I couldn't tell how much he understood; the waking world was so different.

"It's... it's kind of hard to explain," I said.

"Interesting," said the hawk.

"What do I do now?" I asked. "Do I go and find the right places to put the other stones?"

"You will – but first, you must connect with the element of air."

That sounded like a strange thing to do – after all, air was all around me, all the time.

"How?" I asked, awkwardly, wondering if it was something I was already supposed to know.

"Kneel at the direction stone of the east and tell me what you feel."

Kahu hopped to the side and I knelt down in front of the direction stone boulder, bowing my head towards the glowing yellow river stone on top of it. It began to shine brighter.

I closed my eyes.

"Allow your mind to relax, place your hand on the stone, and let it speak to you."

I reached up, placing my hand against the cool surface of the boulder.

Out of nowhere gust of wind rushed past me, bringing with it...

"It feels like... a clear mind," I said. "I can kind of see... ideas – thoughts, lots of them, dancing around..."

"Yes," Kahu said. "Air is of the mind – of focus and intellect. Now tell me, Dreamweaver, how do you connect with this element. What does it mean to you?"

The mind... intellect...

"I don't feel very smart," I said. "My parents were both really good at school and they expect me to be too... but I'm just trying to get through it."

"Is school an intelligent place?" Kahu asked.

I laughed. "Sometimes it can be quite stupid," I said, "but I guess the point is to focus – to learn stuff. It's *supposed* to be intelligent."

"And yet it makes you feel disconnected from your own intellect," the bird mused. "How peculiar... although I must say, we can learn a lot about something by disconnecting from it."

"Okay..." I said, not a hundred per cent sure what he meant.

"Tell me, Dreamweaver, how do you feel about your thoughts and the way they work? How do you feel about your own mind?"

The first thing that occurred to me was *anxiety.*

All those thoughts – swirling around, the tightness in my chest...

Wind began to blow around me.

"What was it you were thinking there?" Kahu asked.

I tried to explain it to him.

"Ah – a storm of the mind – yes, I am familiar with such things."

"You are?" I asked, forgetting that I was supposed to be focused on the stones and looking up at him.

"Yes – for they are all parts of the element of air – and I am the guardian here."

I focused back on the stone.

"Now," Kahu said, "bring to mind a time when you have been strongly focused and it felt good."

I thought of playing online games, and then I thought of reading – of the words and meanings rushing through my mind – of the images appearing, the characters becoming real to me. I felt another blast of air.

"Excellent," Kahu said when I explained it to him. "And such an interesting concept… this 'reading'."

I smiled.

"Dreamweaver, I can tell that you have some mastery already over the element of air – you have focus and great intelligence regardless of what they say at this 'school'."

I smiled again. Kahu was clearly enjoying thinking about all the waking-life concepts I had told him about.

"You may progress on from here," the hawk said, "but before you go, remember the journey is long and dark – the entrance to the Labyrinth was close to the stone of the east, but to get to the other direction stones requires travelling to the far corners of the realm underground. I cannot warn you of what you will encounter because it is a mystery to me. I only burrow as far as this stone, myself… but I do warn you that there will be danger ahead; allow the sharpness of your mind to help you and protect you."

I nodded.

"Thank you," I said, and turned to go.

"Wait," said Kahu. "I have a gift for you,"

He turned his head back and plucked a single feather, holding it out to me in his beak.

I reached forward to take it.

"Thank you," I said. The feather was light in my hand: light and special and powerful.

"Let my gift support you and remind you that you are not without power, and when you reach the centre stone, place it there."

I thanked Kahu again, wondering what he meant by the 'centre stone'.

I tucked the feather into the little bag Veila had given me with the berries and walked into the dark.

As I walked on Kahu called out, "Remember Dreamweaver: the Labyrinth – many twists and turns. Keep a hand on the wall to keep your orientation strong."

I kept walking deeper into the Labyrinth, through the dusty stale air. I could only just see one step in front of me at the time through the light of the river stones. As I walked, stones, dust, and dry dirt crumbled from the walls. *At any moment the entire thing could collapse and trap me here...*

But I did my best to pull my thoughts back from anxiety – to centre myself.

One step in front of another.

It was reassuring to think that it was just a dream – that I would wake up and be back in the light – away from the oppressive darkness. But I knew that my dreams could hurt me... and there was no way of knowing if I would ever make it out of here alive.

Every step was a risk. I didn't know what danger might lie ahead. I couldn't see anything. The path became rougher under my feet. I tried to summon light, but it didn't work.

I feared the path would give-way under my feet – that I would fall...

Maybe my Dreamweaver powers don't work in here.

That was how it was, night after night, walking in the dark.

The only thing I could see was the faint glow of the stones in my pocket, everything else was absolute darkness. I kept my hand against the right side of the Labyrinth. The further I walked, the deeper my sense of dread grew.

Will I ever get out of here?

I would wake in the morning feeling like I had just run a marathon. Mum kept asking me if I was alright. It was hard to pay attention at school because I was so tired.

"I think you might have caught a bug at that camp," Mum said.

She let me stay home from school for a few days, which meant I could sleep even more – and walk even deeper into the Labyrinth. I didn't meet anyone else for a few nights.

I rationed the berries Veila had given me, knowing

there was a much longer journey ahead. I hadn't even gotten to the second direction stone yet. Each berry was a small, sweet delight, bringing in hope and joy, but soon the nice feelings would fade – eclipsed by the darkness of the Labyrinth.

I wish I could just escape this...

So many times I wanted just to stop dreaming in the darkness but I knew I couldn't go back to the Grove or to the meadow, not until I had completed my quest. I could only dream into the Labyrinth if I said the charm, or the Rooms of Mind if I didn't. I tried teleporting a few times but Veila was right: nothing seemed to work down here. The only way out was to walk back – undoing everything I had done so far and making even more work for myself.

There's no escape.

I felt trapped, but I knew I just needed to carry on.

A glow up ahead!

After what felt like an eternity, I could finally see... something.

I moved faster towards the faint light.

Tree roots.

I could see them, twisting around the side of the Labyrinth path, glowing faintly with light that came from an unknown source.

There was something familiar about the tree roots in front of me, and as I neared them I realised why.

Hello Dreamweaver, said the familiar voice, in my mind. It was the Priestess Tree.

"Hello," I said aloud. It was the first time I had seen

her in person, rather than just in my mind. She was even more beautiful, glowing softly in that dark passageway; serene, as if carved out of wood, her hair made of small twisted tree roots, flowing back from her head. Her eyes stayed closed.

It was great to finally find a friend after so many nights in the dark.

"Are you a guardian?" I asked. "Am I at the next direction stone?"

No, the Priestess Tree replied. *You still have some way to go to get to my sister in the north, and you must hurry!*

"Your sister?" I asked, but the Priestess did not elaborate. "I know I have to hurry," I said. "Has the dome cracked open?"

Much has happened in the days you have been gone, Dreamweaver, we are in grave danger. The fragments have escaped and it will not be long until they come for you too.

"What's happening?" I asked, longing to be up there, to be able to help.

We do not know, yet, but we sense something coming, something big.

"I can come back," I said. "I can stop them."

You must place the touchstones at the four quarters of the directions and elements, you must master the elements in yourself, that is the only way you can help.

"But I can fight them," I said, "I can trap them…"

Fighting will only strengthen them, and trapping them can only be temporary, as you have seen. You need mastery of your powers to make lasting change.

I let my shoulders slump in defeat. *But I've already*

gone so far, and there's so much further to go, even just to get to the next stone.

You can move faster, the voice of the Priestess Tree rang out in my head.

"But I can't." I said, "I've tried. The ground is too uneven to run, and I can't use my Dreamweaver powers in here – I can't even light up the darkness…"

Trust, the Priestess Tree replied. *You may move faster if you trust the process. Close your eyes and feel yourself, guided by the pull of the Labyrinth. Keep your hand along the side of the wall so that you may stay on your path. Go now, Dreamweaver. There is no time to spare.*

I said goodbye and turned back to the direction I was walking in. It was so dark ahead – a total void – but the thought of closing my eyes was terrifying.

Trust, I thought, *in what?*

In your own ability, and in life's ability to provide for you, the Priestess Tree continued to read my mind.

Okay… I can do this.

I closed my eyes in the complete darkness, bracing myself in case of attack.

Relax, said the Tree, *you will never get anywhere if you don't relax.*

I slowed my breathing.

Trust, let go, relax…

I felt my feet lifting slightly off the ground, and the air moving past me.

It's working!

I was gliding deeper and deeper into the Labyrinth;

I knew that every inch I travelled into the dark was still a risk – but it was a risk I needed to take.

I worried about bumping into something – or someone. I didn't know what kinds of dangerous things might be lurking in the dark. Every time I braced myself in fear I would slow down again.

Trust...

I relaxed and sped up. *Okay, I get it.*

I relaxed so much that I did not notice the faint glow behind my eyelids until...

"Rarrr!"

I just about jumped out of my skin in shock.

I opened my eyes to bright orange light. I leapt backwards.

Fire!

As my eyes adjusted I saw that it was no ordinary fire. A bright red man stood in front of me. It looked like flames were shooting out of his head. His eyes blazed with rage.

What the...

"Oi! You!" he snarled. "You're coming with me!"

"What?" I said, still shocked and confused. "I don't think so."

"Oh yes... yes, you are. Those are my orders, whether you like it or not."

He reached out for me and I jumped back.

"What's your problem?" I yelled.

"You are! – you're everything that's wrong with this place."

That sounded familiar. It was exactly the kind of thing that Judgement or the Politician would say. I knew where his orders must be coming from. Now it was my turn to rage.

Those vile creatures are at it again. I bet they are doing awful things up above in the Dreamrealm. How dare they? The better not hurt my friends.

"No way!" I said. "I'm not coming with you. Get out of my way."

My rage was stronger than my fear, no matter how freaky this fiery red guy was.

He stood there for a moment, and we both glared at each other.

Something else caught my eye. I glanced down to see the red stone glowing brighter and brighter.

"Wait," said the man. "What's what in your pocket?"

His voice still sounded angry but I could tell he was scared, too. I reached into my pocket and held the stone out.

"Get that... thing... away from me!" he yelled.

I stepped forward.

"It will be far, far away from you if you get far away from me!" I cried.

I started to chase him with the stone, and as I did, he grew brighter and brighter until he disappeared into a giant puff of smoke.

I coughed, fanning the smoke away from my face.

Well... that was weird. I guess that angry man was another fragment, and he's probably gone back to tell the others that he's seen me in the Labyrinth.

I continued down the path, the red stone glowing brighter and brighter in my hand.

As I went on, the walls of the Labyrinth started to change and I noticed more tree roots, which twisted around a brightly glowing boulder – the boulder flickered in red and orange, like flames.

I held the stone up towards the boulder and it glowed even brighter.

The next direction stone! But where is the guardian?

As I reached out towards the boulder, ready to place the stone on it, I steadied myself with my other hand against the tree roots.

The view in front of me was replaced with a wide indigo ocean, sparkling in the sunlight under the swirling purple sky. I could hear seagulls in the distance. I was above ground again, somehow. My hand rested against the trunk of a mighty tree. I looked up and recognised the bright red fluffy flowers of the pohutukawa.

Welcome Dreamweaver, a voice in my head sounded. It was like the Priestess Tree but older and deeper.

I am Pohutukawa, guardian of the north and of fire.

"Uhh, hello," I said, "why are we above the ground now?"

I am showing you my home, the tree said.

"It's beautiful," I replied. I had missed being in the upper dream world, in the sun, where everything seemed to glow with its own light. I looked behind me to find forest stretching out as far as I could see. It was probably the same forest that the Grove was in, just far,

far away. I wondered if Veila was there, waiting for me to complete my quest in the Labyrinth. I wondered where the fragments where, and whether they could have captured Veila by now. My chest tightened in fear.

You may return, said the tree and I was back underground again. I sighed, wishing I could be out of here.

Place the stone onto the boulder – the direction stone of the north, said Pohutukawa in my head.

I reached forward and carefully united the small red stone with the much larger one. A bright light glowed between them as if they were communicating.

Now you must connect with the element of fire...

I closed my eyes and knelt in front of the stones like I had done for the element of air in the east.

To master fire you must know the parts of yourself that burn with it... your passions, your creativity, expression, energy... even anger.

"How do I do that?" I said. I knew I had a lot of anger – mostly at Felicity, and at my parents when they were being annoying, but I wasn't sure about the other stuff.

Cup your hands together, in front of you.

I did as I was told.

Now imagine the sparks of all the strong motivations and drives – the things you really care about, and the strength of those things. Allow them to each be sparks in the palm of your hand.

I thought about reading, and my friends, Ella, Evan and Veila, and how much I cared about them, and my parents, Aunty Rosetta and Nannie. Tiny sparks appeared in the palm of my hand.

Now think about the times you have enjoyed creation – to build or make something, or to move or express yourself...

I thought about the times at my old school where we had made things out of clay. I had enjoyed it so much more than the other kids, even though it was mucky. Another spark appeared in my hands. I remembered the time we had a debate at school and I had made the best arguments. It had felt so good to express myself and be listened to... more and more examples flooded in and my hands were full of tiny flames.

Now, you must learn to master rage. Imagine all those precious things being taken from you.

I felt a burning sensation in my chest and the flames in my hand erupted into burning fire.

"No!" It was too much. I hurled it at the wall.

That was a good attempt, Dreamweaver. We have made much progress. Now, repeat what we just did. You must learn to sit peacefully with the anger and rage to truly master fire.

"Do I have to?" I asked. I was still trembling with fear from the blast of flames – fear that I could set the tree guardian on fire. I wondered why on earth a tree would be a guardian for fire anyway, when they are so obviously flammable.

Ha, ha, ha! I could hear Pohutukawa laugh in my mind, finding my thoughts hilarious. I wished these trees would stop being so ridiculously telepathic already! More laughter.

"Okay," I said, after I had calmed down. "I'm ready to try again."

It took a few more attempts to get to the point where I could sit with the burning rage and the fire in my hands without dropping it or hurling it at the wall, but finally, I got there, only to wake up in my bed with very sweaty sheets.

CHAPTER TWENTY-ONE

I felt a bit lighter the next day. I went to school but still found it hard to concentrate. As I was packing up, I noticed Felicity standing by the cubbies. I tried my best to ignore her. I put my school stuff into my cubby and turned to leave. Felicity smiled at me which made me feel awful – like I better watch out.

I couldn't wait to get out of there.

I went home, feeling exhausted, and got straight into bed. Luckily it was a habit now to say Veila's charm in my head as I fell asleep.

I arrived back into the darkness of the Labyrinth, standing next to Pohutukawa.

Well done, Dreamweaver, Pohutukawa said. *My sister was right about you... you are brave and strong and bright. You bring me great hope.*

"Thank you," I said, blushing at the compliments. "I better go now – I've really got to get to the other direction stones so I can protect my friends from the fragments!"

I understand, said Pohutukawa. *Before you go, hold out your hands.*

I cupped my hands in front of me, raising them up towards the tree. I heard a slight rustling sound and watched as a bright red flower fell from somewhere in the tangle of roots above, landing perfectly in the palms of my hands.

"Thanks," I said, tucking the flower into the bag with the feather from Kahu.

I closed my eyes and relaxed again, so that I could glide through the Labyrinth, much faster than I could walk. I knew I had travelled quite far, but I had no way of knowing how close I was to the next direction stone.

I kept going, occasionally eating one of Veila's berries to boost my energy, as I glided along the dark passageway. I kept my hand trailing against the right wall to make sure I didn't accidentally lose my way in the winding pathways of the Labyrinth, where I could be lost forever.

The stones in my pocket were not glowing any brighter than usual – so it surprised me to see a blurry glow up ahead. I was going so fast that I couldn't stop in time. I collided with something soft, and damp. There was a splash of water and then…

"Ouch," a voice said. I heard sobbing.

As my eyes adjusted to the faint blue glow of light I saw a small child.

She was sitting on the ground in a puddle of water, tears running down her cheeks.

"I'm sorry," I said. The girl couldn't have been more than six years old, based on her size.

"No, you're not sorry. No one ever is; no one cares about me…" She sobbed and wailed.

"What's your name?" I asked, feeling sorry for this small being, stuck down here in the Labyrinth. I realised she could be a fragment. It could even be a trap; but she seemed so sad sitting there, cold and alone.

"A name?" the child said. "I don't have a name; no one ever bothered to give me a name – and why would they, when all I do is cry."

"That's sad," I said, looking around and remembering I had no time to spare.

"Look," I said, "I have to get going…"

"Of course you do," she sobbed, "just like everyone else – you're too busy for me. I'll just stay here and cry some more."

I shrugged. "You could come with me if you like," I offered. I did still wonder if that was a safe thing for me to suggest but she seemed so helpless.

"You don't mean that," she replied. "No one wants to be with me. No one ever does…" She broke down into even more sobs and loud wailing.

I knew I needed to go but I couldn't just leave her there alone by herself.

"No – look – " I looked around, desperate to try to find something that would distract her from her crying. *Maybe the next guardian can help...* "Actually…" I said. "I think I know someone who might be able to help – they are very wise and maybe… maybe they can give you a name."

The child stopped sobbing, considering my words.

"Okay," she said, finally. "I'll come with you."

She stood up from what I realised was probably a puddle of her own tears. More tears continued to trickle down her cheeks as she walked slowly next to me.

"Do you know how to move fast?" I asked.

The child shook her head.

"How about I carry you?" I offered. I had no idea if I could actually carry her and glide at the same time, but it was worth a try.

The child nodded and reached up to me. She wasn't heavy. I propped her on my hip, closed my eyes and we began to move. I could feel tears falling down my arm as we went, but I didn't mind too much. I felt sorry for this little girl, even if she was a fragment – she just needed someone to look after her.

"What's that?" she said.

I could hear the sound of running water. I slowed down and opened my eyes to see bright blue water, flowing right down the side of the Labyrinth wall into a pool to the side of the path.

"It's beautiful," I said, putting the girl down and walking more slowly towards the sound.

"So beautiful…" said the child next to me, who began to cry even more.

I noticed the water spilt over a big boulder, similar to the other direction stones. I looked down to see my pocket glowing blue and I reached in to retrieve the blue river stone.

"What's that?" the child said, in wonder.

"It's a special stone... I think this is the stone for the element of water," I said, "but where is the guardian?"

"Who?" she asked.

"The guardian... I'm going to ask the guardian of water to give you a name."

I stepped closer to the water. A pink shimmer caught my eye and disappeared – it was familiar. I tried to think of where I had seen it before... *that's right... I saw the same thing in the pool in the Grove... but we must be miles from there.*

"Hello?" I said, moving even closer to the water. I reached my hand out and let the water run over my fingers. It shimmered and glowed at my touch.

"Wow!" said the child, moving closer to my side.

"Welcome, Dreamweaver."

I looked around but I couldn't tell where the strange silky voice was coming from. The child backed up against the opposite side of the Labyrinth wall, eyes wide.

"Hello?" I said. "Where are you?"

"Down here."

I looked down to see a gleaming pink fish shimmering with surreal rainbow, sparkly scales, poking his head out of the water.

"Uhhh, umm... hi," I said, trying to mask my surprise.

"Welcome to the west and the element of water. I am the Salmon of Wisdom and it is my task to guard over this direction stone."

Salmon of Wisdom! I giggled internally, hoping the salmon couldn't read my mind like the trees could.

"Nice to meet you," I said, trying to be polite, even though the situation was so very odd.

"And you too, Dreamweaver. I can tell you think I'm funny – a salmon of wisdom... but I'll have you know, the salmon are sacred to your father's, father's, people."

"Who?" I asked, "...the Scottish?"

"That's right," said the salmon. "And I see you have brought a friend."

The child stepped forward, staring in awe at the talking pink fish. "Friend?" she said.

The tears stopped flowing for a moment.

She looked up at me and said, "So, you are the Dreamweaver."

I smiled and nodded.

Worry flashed in the child's eyes. She stood back against the wall again, shivering and crying.

"What is it?" I asked.

"The Dreamweaver is foretold to come here and destroy us."

"What?" I asked. "No – I don't want to destroy anything. I'm just trying to help."

The child shook her head. "No one wants to help

us," she said. "We are just splinters – we are incomplete. There is no helping us."

So I was right... she is a fragment, I realised, *but she seems so sad and harmless.*

"I don't want to hurt you," I said. "I'm your friend, remember – we came here to ask the guardian for a name for you." I turned to the salmon. "Can you help?"

The salmon swirled around in the pool a few times and then came back up to the surface. "Come closer, child."

The child walked cautiously to the edge of the pool.

"Put your hand into the water of the west pool."

She followed the salmon's instructions. The water glowed white and rippled outwards.

"Ah – I see your name is *Roimata*."

"Roimata," the child repeated, rolling the 'r' and lengthening the 'ah' sounds just as the salmon had done.

"That's a beautiful name," I said. It sounded familiar, but I didn't know where I had heard it before. A memory swam back into my mind, me sitting with Aunty Rosetta by the fire in Kāwhia. *Tears, connection, remembrance...* the words rang through my mind.

I wanted to put all that into a form Roimata would understand but I didn't want to upset her by telling her that her name meant "tears." *Maybe I can look it up later and explain the meaning to her...*

"See, now you have a name – and you don't have to be sad anymore."

Roimata lifted her hands to her eyes and rubbed them, even more tears seemed to pour out.

"Hey – it's okay," I said.

"No – you misunderstand," Roimata replied. "These are tears of joy; they are beautiful. I've never had happy tears before. Thank you."

I reached down and wrapped my arms around her to hug her. Bright light flashed around and through us.

She was gone.

I stood alone in the tunnel.

"Remarkable," said the salmon.

"Where has she gone?" I asked, looking around in worry.

"You have alchemised her."

"No!" I yelled, "I said I would help her – and she trusted me."

"Oh, but you have helped her, Dreamweaver – more than you know."

I felt a surge of anger. This fish didn't understand at all.

"I *killed* her," I said, "It's just like she said – she was warned about me."

"That is where you have misunderstood, Dreamweaver. She is not dead; you have killed no one."

"But she was *someone*," I said. "She had a name…"

"And she still does. You will see in time."

I sighed, hoping the salmon was right, but I couldn't shake the feeling of sadness at the reality of losing the friend I had just met.

I looked down and noticed I still held the river stone in my hand, glowing bright blue.

"I guess I need to put this on the boulder now..."

The salmon nodded.

I climbed into the west pool, which came up to just above my knees; the cool water around my legs calmed me. I waded to the boulder and placed the blue stone on top, it seemed to click into place and both stones began to glow.

I bowed my head and crouched down into the water.

"What are you doing now?" the salmon asked me.

"Shouldn't you know? I said. "I need to learn about the element of water – just like with the other stones."

"Ahh," the salmon said. "It is clear to me from what I just saw that you already have mastery over the element of water. You are connected with your feelings, which makes you wise beyond your years, and helps you to see so much more than other people can – but tell me: what is it that you experience now?"

I could feel the water all around me – connected to the rivers and to the ocean, pulled by the sun and moon – the same water that lives in every creature – that makes up most of the human body – I could feel it in my cells, in my mouth, in my blood.

"Water is life..." I said. "Water is emotion – feeling – caring..."

"Yes," said the salmon. "Sometimes one element is stronger in people than other times, and for you, water is your strength. That is why you are so powerful in this work, and why you can achieve mastery so quickly... you can feel your way through the dark of the unknown. This is why you have already alchemised a fragment, even before you have reached the centre of the Labyrinth – when you are still so young. It took the last Dreamweaver many years to achieve such mastery."

I left the pool and prepared to leave.

"Wait," said the salmon. "I have a gift for you."

I held out my hands and received a small blue shell.

"Thank you," I said, and continued on, into the dark. I felt confused. The salmon had been so nice to me but I felt bad about Roimata. She had trusted me and I had... *I'd alchemised her.*

I'd thought I wanted to alchemise the fragments because they were dangerous, but maybe I had it all wrong. *Maybe I'm the dangerous one...*

The swirling confusion drifted away and was replaced by more soothing feelings.

There had been a flash of light and a boost of energy. Something inside me told me not to be too sad. *She's not really gone, she can't be... alchemising just means connecting back with the 'whole' – whatever that means.*

And with that thought, I woke up.

CHAPTER TWENTY-TWO

*E*lla and Evan were sitting together in the courtyard as I walked into school that morning. I had enough on my plate with all the weird stuff happening in the Labyrinth, and besides, I didn't want to bother them so I waved when they saw me and kept walking. My anxiety thoughts started again:

I'm sure they don't want me intruding on their time... they're always together... and I'm left out. I guess I'm alone again with no friends. Who would want to be my friend anyway... when I'm obviously such a freak? They've probably figured out by now that there's something wrong with me.

The world around me started going grey, but I didn't care anymore.

"Hey," Ella said, running up to me as I got close to the main door. "What's wrong? Why didn't you come and sit with us?"

"It's nothing," I said. "I've just got a lot on my mind

and I'm sure you don't want me around being a third wheel."

"Not this again," Ella said.

"What?" I asked. "I didn't think you had time for me anymore."

Ella recoiled at my words as if they'd cut her. She crossed her arms and said, "Well it seems like *you* never have time for *us*."

That surprised me. *I guess I have been so tired lately, and so focussed on my dream life that I haven't been paying attention to my waking life friends. I guess I've been protecting myself – waiting for them to give up on me.*

"I'm sorry," I said, "I just assumed you two didn't want to hang out with me anymore so I was making it easy for you."

"Awa, how many times do I have to tell you? You're my best friend. Of course, I want to hang out with you. I just wish you didn't keep catastrophising – assuming the worst! It's like anxiety makes you think everything's the flipping end of the world!"

As her words sunk in, I realised she had a point.

"You're right," I said. "I think it is the anxiety... I keep thinking that you and Evan are going to leave me out – because, well there was that whole thing with crushes... and I don't really understand any of it. First Evan had a crush on me a while ago, and then I found out you had a crush on him, and then there was all this stuff with both of you liking each other... I told you before, I don't get crushes... like maybe there's something wrong with me..."

"There's nothing wrong with you, Awa," Ella said. "Crushes are actually a pain, and everyone is different. I'm sure there are heaps of people in the world who don't – I mean, haven't you ever googled it?"

"I did once," I admitted. "I found all this stuff about something called 'ace spectrum' but I've never met anyone else like that... at least I don't think I have."

"It sounds like a totally legit thing to be," Ella said. "Like, it's fine if that's how you are, and it's also fine if you do start getting crushes... either way I think you're special and I'll still want to be your friend. There is nothing wrong with you, okay?"

"I guess," I said, feeling embarrassed for making such a big deal about it.

"Me and Evan are just friends, Awa," Ella said, "... and even if we were more than that, we'd both still want to be your friend, and hang out with you lots, so please stop freaking out, if you can."

There was a moment of silence before I could look Ella in the eyes again, knowing she was right. I was relieved to see her smile.

We both laughed. And again, more than ever, I wished I could tell her about the Dreamrealm.

The bell rang and we walked to class together. Evan made silly jokes about how I was always giving up on them and we laughed.

As I was getting my stationary out of my cubby, I overheard Felicity telling Mr Jasper that something had been stolen from her.

I reached into my cubby and felt something unfamiliar, it was a small cylinder. I pulled it out, only to realise it was the pink Valerie Sparkles lip gloss – Felicity's lip gloss!

I tried to tuck it away before Felicity and Mr Jasper noticed, but Felicity's voice interrupted me:

"There it is! Awa has it! She stole it from me!"

"Is this true, Awa?" Mr Jasper asked.

I froze.

"No... I mean..." I fumbled over my words, and a confession came tumbling out of my mouth before I could stop it. "I... I did..."

I felt like I couldn't breathe. The room around me was turning grey. What had just come out of my mouth? Everyone was looking at me. Everything was wrong and it was too late to take it back. *Just relax...* a calm voice in my head said. *It will all be okay.*

I didn't believe that. How could it possibly be okay? How had I been so stupid to admit to something... even if it was kind of true. I knew I needed to speak but I had no idea what to say.

"I did take the lip-gloss..." I said. "I mean... but not here... not now..."

Mr Jasper raised his eyebrows.

"How is it that you came to be holding it in your hand, then, Awa?"

"I don't know..."

My mind was racing even faster than my heart.

Felicity...

I looked over at her smirking face.

Felicity was standing by the cubbies yesterday. She framed me.

"It was her," I said, pointing at Felicity. "She did this, and she's not even supposed to have make-up at school!"

Felicity's face twisted into a scowl.

"Stealing is wrong, Awa," she said. "You're in so much trouble."

"You're the one who should be in trouble you horrible bullying rat!"

"You're the rat!" Felicity yelled. "You're the one who's always ruining everything – you're such an attention-seeking loser!"

Our voices were raised so loud now that I could barely hear Mr Jasper yell: "STOP!"

We both stopped. The whole class was staring. My breath caught in my throat; the blood rushed to my head, but things weren't going grey around me for a change; it was more like bright red fire was burning in my veins.

I wasn't anxious, I was just angry!

"Detention for both of you," Mr Jasper said.

My anger turned from bright red to black.

"That's not fair," Felicity and I said at the same time.

"Well, hopefully it will teach you both a lesson," Mr Jasper said.

The rest of the day was a blur. I kept mulling over the same thoughts: *What's Dad going to think... what's Mum going to say? I'm sure she'd be mad at Mr Jasper for giving me detention with the racist girl... although to be fair Felicity hadn't said anything racist since Mum had called her out in front of the whole school. I hate it when Mum's right.*

I had never had detention before. It totally took my mind off the Dreamrealm and the Labyrinth and everything else. I did *not* want to disappoint my parents – no matter how much they disappointed me on a daily basis.

Detention was after school. Mr Jasper gave us a plastic bag and told us to pick up rubbish off the field for an hour – or until we had filled the entire bag.

"Work together," he said. "It will be much faster that way – and I expect any students in my class to be able to work together without fighting."

He gave us a meaningful look and I knew I'd been right in my guess that Mr Jasper put us in the same cabin on purpose. He wanted us to sort out our difficulties and learn to get along. *Like that will ever happen in a million years!*

I knew co-operating was the only way to get out of this without getting into even deeper trouble.

"Okay," I said, taking the bag. Felicity still had her arms crossed.

"I'll be in over here, catching up on my reading," Mr Jasper said, "so make sure you are *both* picking up rubbish."

He was looking at Felicity but she was staring at the ground.

As soon as Mr Jasper turned his back, Felicity walked away.

"Aren't you going to help?" I said, bending down to pick up a bread tag from the grass.

"Oh fine," she said, "give me that."

She snatched the bag out of my hand.

Typical Felicity... I thought, but then I remembered how kind her mother had been to me at school camp.... And how innocent she had looked the time that I had gone in search of Veila and accidentally landed in Felicity's bedroom that night.

"I honestly don't get it," I said.

"Get what?" Felicity asked, pouting.

"Your Mum is so nice. She helped me when I couldn't get back to the cabins at camp... I don't get why you are so mean."

"You try having a dad who controls everything and an older sister who is perfect, and a brother who teases you and tries to flush you in the toilet all the time!" Felicity yelled. Her cheeks had gone red and she was crying.

"I didn't know," I said... *so Felicity gets bullied too,* I realised. *She gets bullied by her brother and she's never as good at anything as her sister is... that's why she's always wanting to be in control... that's why she wants everything to be perfect...*

"Mum's fine," Felicity continued ranting, waving her hands in the air, "but she never stands up to Dad or Mitch, and she pays the most attention to my sister. Dad says he's teaching us how the real-world works. You have to pick a weakness and then turn it to your advantage."

Felicity stopped talking, and blushed, as if she hadn't meant to say any of that.

"Why though?" I asked. "What's the point?"

"To win," said Felicity, "...obviously."

"But what's the point of winning if everyone else loses?"

Felicity shrugged and continued picking up rubbish.

Something had changed between us, and I wasn't sure what it was. We were never going to be friends, but maybe we weren't enemies anymore either.

It didn't take long for us to fill up the bag, working together, especially with all the rubbish in the garden beds next to the driveway. It wasn't even that bad, and it was kind of satisfying – handing Mr Jasper the bag after only twenty minutes, and seeing his surprised smile.

I got home, and Mum was already there, standing in the hallway with her arms crossed.

"What?" I said.

"Detention?" Mum replied. "Really, Awa!"

"It wasn't my fault!" I said, pushing past her towards the kitchen to get a glass of water.

"I knew you were having a hard time, Awa," Mum said, "...but I never suspected you of stealing,"

"Mum – I told you! It wasn't my fault!" I said, accidentally spilling water from my glass all over my top.

"Really?" Mum said. "Then how do you explain this?"

Mum held up my jewellery box, opening it to

reveal the things I had taken from her room – the things Dad had given her. It felt like lead was churning in my guts.

"You went into my room!" I yelled.

"What was I supposed to do when the school called to tell me you'd been stealing?"

"You could have just asked," I snapped, glaring at Mum. I wanted to get away from her but I knew she wouldn't leave me alone until she was finished with whatever rant she had prepared about me getting into trouble again.

"How can I trust you?" Mum asked. "How can I trust someone who goes through my jewellery and takes things?"

"You don't deserve them," I said.

"Excuse me?" said Mum.

"Dad gave you those things," I said, trying to hold back the tears as my throat tightened around the words.

"Honey," Mum said.

She sat down on the edge of the bed and put her arms around me. "You should have just asked…. I know you're missing him…"

"I was worried you were going to throw them out," I said, tears flowing down my face. "I thought if I asked, you might remember that they were there and get rid of them."

Mum sat with me for a while, and I told her the whole story – about the jewellery, and about the lip-gloss and how I had kind of taken it at camp and then put it back – and how Felicity had put it in my cubby to frame me.

"That girl is a real piece of work," Mum said, reminding me of how she had made Felicity apologise for bullying me in front of the whole school. This time, instead of feeling embarrassed, I felt kind of proud of Mum and how she stuck up for me and stood her ground.

"Dad will be home from his big business trip in a few weeks, love," Mum said, "and I'll make sure there are lots of opportunities for you two to spend time together."

"Thanks, Mum," I said, and I hugged her back.

As we pulled away from each other I remembered what Aunty Rosetta had told me, about my mum having a similar 'gift' to me. Rosetta had called it 'second sight.'

I wanted to ask Mum about it. I wanted to be able to tell her about my dream-life. But then I remembered how weird she had been about my dreams when I used to talk about them…. and Rosetta had told me how much Mum's gift had scared her.

Mum smiled at me and I knew I didn't want to ruin the moment by bringing up things that might freak her out. She was finally happy with me again.

Maybe one day I can tell her... and maybe one day I can tell my friends too.

CHAPTER TWENTY-THREE

I heard their voices as I was falling asleep that night: Veila. Honu. The Priestess Tree.

Hurry Dreamweaver – we do not have much time.

We are trying to hold them off.

Help... we need your help...

Their voices mixed and mingled together, and echoed into the dark pathway of the Labyrinth. I had no idea what was going on above. How could I? I'm stuck down here, in the dark, until I place all these freaking stones. I reached into my pocket and realised there was only one stone left, aside from the seer's stone.

I'm almost there!

I closed my eyes and willed myself to move along the dark path as fast as possible, carefully keeping my right hand trailing along the wall of the Labyrinth. I didn't even care what kind of dangers might be right in front of me – I needed to help my friends more than I feared the unknown risks of the Labyrinth.

I could tell I was speeding along very fast by the feel of the air rushing past me. I ate one of the last berries in my little bag for a boost of energy, remembering how Veila had so thoughtfully picked them for me. I'm coming, Veila.

I sped, faster and faster until…

Crash!

I collided with something hard and solid – right in front of me, which sent me flying backward.

"What the…?"

I opened my eyes and looked around. The only light came from the stone glowing green in my hand, but I couldn't see anything else around me. I lifted my right hand, searching for the familiar wall, but all I felt was the thick air of the Labyrinth brush my fingertips.

I must have been turned around by the impact of crashing into whatever that was before.

I moved my arms in a circle, hoping to find the familiar texture of the wall of the Labyrinth, but there was nothing to grasp…

I'm lost!

What if I've been completely turned around and I have to head all the way back to the last direction stone?

What if I'm on some other wrong pathway leading me somewhere completely different?

A sound broke through, as if a large animal was scraping the ground, followed by a low bellow.

I backed away, slowly, until I felt the familiar wall of the Labyrinth brush up behind me. It was hard to stop my thoughts from imagining awful monsters that might be lurking in the shadows.

Okay... think...

I need to centre myself... obviously.

I slowed my breathing. Realising that whatever made that noise was not following me. I managed to calm down enough that my mind cleared.

Maybe the seer's stone can help me.

I held it close to the glowing green stone, trying to illuminate the surface. I relaxed my mind and watched the smooth side of the seer's stone shimmer and swirl. Images danced across the stone, and then settled and became clear. I recognised a familiar face. Honu! The giant turtle looked as if he was underwater, he smiled at me and I could tell he knew I was here.

"Honu, I need your help!" I whispered. "I'm all alone in the dark labyrinth and I've got no sense of direction. I crashed into something and I lost contact with the wall. I don't know which way to go, and there's a scary sounding animal or something in here with me."

I heard Honu's voice in my mind.

Where there is darkness you'll find light

"But I can't. The darkness is too thick."

Be your own light... You have the power

"I don't have much power in here."

What does light feel like? Focus on the feeling and you will find a way.

I closed my eyes and focussed on the feeling of bright light – of lightness. Something started glowing. I opened my eyes to see the seer's stone shining bright light, illuminating the Labyrinth pathway around me.

I looked in the direction of the animal noise from before.

I saw two horns and my gut tightened. But as my eyes adjusted to the light I realised what it was. Standing in front of me, blocking a narrow part of the passageway, was a huge bull.

It slowly opened its eyes and looked at me.

"Uhh, hello," I said, trying to be friendly.

The bull puffed air through its nostrils and shifted its feet slightly.

"Umm… hi… are you… do you happen to know… are you the guardian of earth, by chance?" I asked, finally.

The bull looked at me and glared.

"No," it said, in a deep, rich voice.

"Oh, okay… well, if you don't mind… I need to get past… it's kind of urgent… could you please just… just shift to the side a bit?"

The bull didn't bother looking at me this time.

"No."

Its voice echoed down the dark pathway of the Labyrinth.

"Please?"

"No."

It didn't matter what I said. The answer was always no. *I wonder if this bull is also a fragment… and maybe it's trying to stop me from getting through... or maybe it just doesn't want to move...*

It reminded me of the thing Mum had sometimes said when I refused to listen to her – *stubborn as a bull!*

"In that case," I said, getting desperate, "if I climb around you somehow, will you try to stop me?"

"No," came the answer, exactly the same as before.

It occurred to me that 'no' might be the only word the bull knew, but I had to risk it anyway. I knew I needed to try to get around the bull one way or another. I didn't have time to convince it to move.

There was enough space underneath to crawl but it would be so easy for the bull to trample me by just moving its legs, and I didn't want to give it that opportunity in case it really was out to get me. Instead, I decided to try climbing over its back.

I could only get enough grip by grabbing one of the horns and pulling myself up over its head.

The bull puffed out of its nostrils again and I froze, one leg dangling in the air, scared it was going to buck me off.

After a moment of silence, I kicked my other leg up. I was on top of the bull. It shifted its feet beneath me, pawing the ground as if it was mad but was still too stubborn to move.

I took my opportunity and clambered right over the top of the bull and jumped. I landed on the other side, feeling triumphant. The bull let out a low moan behind me but still did not move.

I looked around. The walls in front of me glowed

green and it took me a while to realise it was because they were all covered in soft green moss. It gleamed with tiny drops of dew in the light coming from a large boulder.

Finally – the last direction stone!

I stepped closer, looking around for the guardian of the north.

The shape of the boulder was irregular, a bit different from the others. As I looked more closely I saw very subtle movement – as if it was beating with a tiny heartbeat.

The boulder began to speak!

"Welcome, Dreamweaver," said a raspy deep voice, "...we have been expecting you."

I squinted at the boulder and realised the irregular pattern on top of it was actually some kind of lizard – perfectly camouflaged with the colour of the rock.

"Uhh, hello," I said.

"I am Tuatara – guardian of the north and of the element of earth."

Once she said it, I could see it was obviously true: this was the endangered native lizard. I hadn't recognised her before. I guess I just wasn't used to seeing one in real life – let alone in a dark dream labyrinth.

Tuatara moved to the side as I stepped closer, holding the glowing green stone in my hand.

"Yes, that's right, place your element stone on the boulder," said Tuatara.

I put the stone down where she had just been

sitting, and stepped back as the green light shone brightly all around me.

I've placed the last stone! I realised. I'm so close!

I pushed worries about Veila and Honu and the Priestess Tree out of my head and knelt in front of the big green glowing rock.

I closed my eyes.

The element of earth felt heavy… but also stable… reliable. I could see the planet earth, constantly moving, solid, full of life – but also so restrictive, so hard and challenging, so limiting – just like that stubborn bull that blocked my path just moments before…

"You must connect to the element of earth in yourself, see it in your own personality, in your own life…" Tuatara said.

Mum always says I'm stubborn… that was about as far as I could make the connection until I remembered how much I love being outside, in the forest, how much I loved collecting rocks and crystals when I was younger. I had such a big collection of them at the old house, but I had to let them go when we moved because there was no room in the apartment – no room for me…

A tear began to trickle down my cheek.

"You are doing a fine job, Dreamweaver," said Tuatara. "You are using your strength in water – in sensing and feelings – to connect with this element too."

I could tell she was right. It was like what the salmon had said. I could feel the element of earth, its solidity, its slowness, its limitations, its constant working towards growing… grounding.

"Well done," Tuatara said.

I opened my eyes and looked at her. She moved, very quickly, back to the boulder.

"I have a gift for you," she said.

I held out my hands, and the lizard placed a small pebble into them. I tucked it into the bag Veila had given me, along with the other gifts.

"Now, you must place your gifts from the elements onto the centre stone," said Tuatara.

"How do I get there?" I asked, looking around, expecting to see a pathway that led directly to the centre of the Labyrinth.

"You must crawl," Tuatara said, gesturing with her small scaly hand towards the opposite wall of the Labyrinth. I looked down and saw a small round opening.

My chest constricted in fear. "Really? Isn't there a bigger path?"

"The centre is a deeper layer, under the earth. Do not fear, your elemental learning will help you as you go, and will strengthen you. Remember, Dreamweaver: to alchemise the fragments we must see them in ourselves – and we must open to them – connect with them – love them."

No!

Everything in me screamed out against that.

I can't love them – they are awful.

I don't want to see them in myself…

I thought of Roimata and how I cared about her because I could relate to her sadness, her tears... b*ut how can I relate to Judgement being so awful... and the Politician with his snake face underneath his nice friendly mask... and all the other scary and stuck fragments...?*

"Be swift, Dreamweaver," Tuatara said.

There was no time to waste.

I reached into the little bag and found the last three berries from Veila. I put them all in my mouth at the same time, savouring their delicious flavours for the boost of courage and energy I needed to get through the strange dark tunnel.

I said goodbye to Tuatara and crouched down in front of the entrance. I could see nothing inside. Nothing at all.

It was just big enough for me to fit through with only a small gap on each side. I began crawling, one hand in front of the other, down, deeper into the earth, feeling the element's solidity and patient stability as I moved.

As I continued on, the air felt even thicker, dustier and staler. My body felt heavier and heavier. I wondered how I could ever make it back out alive... there was no room to turn around now... *what if the path's blocked up ahead?*

Draw on the strength of the elements, Veila's voice sounded in my head.

I focused on each element and tried to imagine what kind of strength it could give me: the passion and drive of fire, the swift analysis of air, the feeling flow of water and the solid determination of earth to keep moving…

When I closed my eyes, I could almost feel each element flicker before it was swallowed up again by the thick darkness.

I could hardly breathe, but what choice did I have?

I recalled how I'd learned to move more quickly through the Labyrinth. I closed my eyes again, relaxing, willing myself to glide.

It works!

I was moving much faster now, I wrapped my arms around my chest; as I sped up the thick air rushed past me.

Faster and faster.

My heart raced in my chest.

Up ahead a light shone, growing bigger and bigger as I got closer.

I tumbled out into a much larger space.

I was sitting in a wide, circular room, still quite dark, but a platform in the centre glowed white.

I looked at it more closely. The top was made of a mosaic of stained glass – an intricate pattern with circles of red, yellow, blue and green: the elemental colours.

I retrieved the four gifts from my bag and placed them onto the centre stone, matching them to the elemental colour of the four circles in the centre: The feather on the yellow circle, because that was the colour of the air river stone, the Pohutukawa flower on the red, the shell on the blue and the pebble from Tuatara on the green.

As I placed the last gift there was a blinding flash of light, followed by loud rumbling. I stood back, shielding my eyes from the light. As it faded I looked back at the centre stone and saw... wow!

Red and blue and yellow and green lights swirled around the table, alchemy in action... they merged together in another bright flash of light. I leaned forward to take a closer look.

In place of the gifts, was an entirely different object.

I stepped closer to examine it. It gleamed silver, shaped like a large circlet, with four points of the front forming a kind of diamond, bearing four gemstones in the colours of the touchstones.

I reached forward. Just as my fingers touched it, the room rumbled around me, and the object disappeared. I felt a coldness tightening around my waist. I looked down to see I was wearing the object – *it's a belt!*

The rumbling intensified. The whole room started to shake. Rocks were crashing down around me. I ducked, but then I noticed my whole body was glowing bright silver. The rocks and stones and dust were falling everywhere, except somehow, miraculously, none of it touched me – even as the whole ceiling caved in.

After the rumbling stopped, I began to climb up the rocks. I could see daylight breaking through where the ceiling had once been and I wanted to be outside more than ever. I pushed myself up through the rubble.

I was standing in the centre of the Dreamrealm, at the edge of the desert. The wind howled and sand whipped around me, but it was so good to see the purple swirling sky above. I reached up towards it, bending my knees, and prepared to fly.

CHAPTER TWENTY-FOUR

*A*s I neared the Priestess Tree I looked over towards the dome that I had trapped the fragments in. The top had clearly burst open, leaving ragged shards of class protruding into the purple sky. Silver slime seemed to be oozing down the outside.

Something strange must have gone on in there.

I landed and approached the Priestess Tree. I wanted to ask her what was going on, and what I could do about it, but just as I got close I heard a deep gurgling sound, followed by…

"Dreamweaver."

I turned to see what looked like a gigantic slug coming towards me. As I looked closer I could tell it was made of the same silvery slime that oozed down the sides of the broken dome. Faces became visible all around it – the faces of the fragments I had trapped in the dome, and some others who they must have gathered together since then... including a few from the Labyrinth!

The face of the slug was clearly recognisable – it was Judgement and she was looking right at me.

They've all fused together into one giant monster...

"How did you escape?" I asked, trying to stall the monster.

Judgement's eyes lit up. She smiled a malicious smile.

"You must have known how powerful we are, Dreamweaver – not only us, but our close friend, the Shadow."

"It took you a while," I said, laughing. I was trying to make the whole thing into a joke, even though my legs were frozen in fear.

"Bow down, Dreamweaver, and submit your powers to us!" the creature said, its many voices speaking at once.

"No!" I said.

"Then we shall destroy you and all you care about!"

The slug creature started moving faster towards me. I tore my legs away from the ground and began to run towards the forest, relieved to feel sheltered and hidden by the trees. I kept running, but as I glanced back I realised the creature was following me – tearing out the trees in its path.

I can't let them destroy the forest. I have to stop. I must be brave...

I tried to think of all I had learned in the Labyrinth

– with each direction and each element... drawing on their strengths, and on the different aspects of myself.

I thought of Roimata, the one fragment I had alchemised so far when I hadn't even known how to... *it had happened because I cared about her...* but how could I care about this big slimy, freaky mess?

I zigzagged back out of the forest to stop the creature from pulling up any more trees, but I knew I needed to stop running – to turn around and face it. I just needed to do it somewhere safe.

I crouched down and leapt into the air, and began flying over the Dreamrealm looking for somewhere – anywhere where there wasn't much to destroy.

I glanced behind me. The gigantic slug was somehow flying – following me – not too far behind. *I have to hurry! But where?*

The desert!

I moved back towards the desert as quickly as I could, conscious of the monster gaining speed behind me. I closed my eyes, willing myself to fly even faster.

I landed near some large sand dunes. The giant slug squelched to the ground a few meters away.

"You can't escape us, Dreamweaver... wherever you go, we will follow."

I knew the monster was right. I had to stop running. I had to face this horrible oozing mess of a creature. I had to be brave.

"I know," I said. "I'm not going to run anymore."

Judgement's eyes lit up.

"So you've finally come to your senses!" she shrieked, triumphant.

"If you want my powers, come and take them," I said.

My voice sounded like a challenge, but my legs were trembling.

It took all the courage I had to stand still and not run away as the freaky oozing mess came closer. It smelled like tar and air-freshener and dead rats.

I tried to hold my breath so I didn't have to breathe in the stench.

The slug was so close by then, I could have reached out and touched its oozy sides. The tip of it, where Judgement's face was, bent down towards me

I wanted to escape – to give up – to wake up.

The pressure of terror in my chest was so intense I felt like I was being squeezed out of my own body.

I reached up, wanting to shield my face…

Judgement.

Memories of her flashed through my mind – how she had chased me, trapped me… how she wanted to destroy things I cared about in order to make things 'better around here'. She had reminded me of Felicity, who had been so nasty to me at school. Then I remembered how Felicity had been during that detention – scared and upset and kind of sad.

Veila's words floated back to me from what felt like a long time ago – *we judge because we are afraid.*

That was it – that was what I needed to focus on:

Empathy.

I connected with the part of myself that was afraid – that judged others…

I understand fear…

Just as Judgement reached down with her slimy arms to grab me, I remembered Roimata again… so instead of hiding, I reached towards her; I pulled her into a hug.

Another blinding flash of light, emanating from my belt.

The tip of the slug burst into silvery-blue energy which hung in the air, swirling into beautiful intricate patterns, before it sank back towards us and was absorbed into the belt and into me.

"What just happened there?" the Politician's voice said, as he rose to the top of the oozing silver sludgy mess. "She's gone?" he asked, with a gleam in his eyes. "Oooh, you don't know how long I've been waiting for this moment!"

He looked at me and smiled his plastic smile, "Now it will all be mine. This is my world now, just waiting for the tall buildings and the big podiums, for my amazing speeches! I just need to get *you* out of the way first."

The Politician removed his mask and the snake slithered out from behind it, towards me. I flinched. My gut churned with fear. I wanted to run away screaming. Then I remembered something Veila had told me a while back: snakes symbolise power.

I needed to be the one with the power here, otherwise what was the point in being a Dreamweaver?

I can do this…

The Politician just wants power and he's willing to lie or do anything else to get it...

There's something so familiar about that...

I thought about all the times I had lied to Mum and Dad... about how I tried to keep my life under control, even if it meant avoiding my friends, about how the things that made me feel out of control, like Felicity, were so awful to deal with... and how sometimes I just wished I could make her go away...

This all comes from fear too, I realised, and after dealing with anxiety for so long, fear was definitely something I could relate to.

As the snake approached me, dripping with slime, I didn't flinch, I reached out towards it, my heart racing as I hugged the Politician, and he evaporated into the same silvery-blue energy.

I felt myself absorbing that too, growing stronger...

The slug began writhing, flinging horrible smelling slime all over the place.

"No!" said a familiar voice. "You will not destroy me – I am special."

A familiar head rose to the top. I recognised the first fragment I had ever met, in one of my early visits to the Dreamrealm. This fragment always insisted on being special and I could feel that part of myself that felt the same way.

I want to be special – but so does everyone else...

"We can all be special," I said, opening my arms again.

"No! No! No!" said the voice, speeding up and

becoming high-pitched. "I'm the special one – I tell you – me – me – me!"

"It's okay," I said, reaching up towards the fragment. I noticed I was floating, without even deliberately trying to…

"There's more than enough," I said. "More than enough attention, and energy, and specialness – you can have all the specialness you need."

I hugged the fragment and it burst into bright blue light.

It was quickly replaced by another familiar face.

"Get away from my stuff!" the hoarder said, as the slug stumbled back, away from me. "It's all mine, I tell you!"

I looked at the hoarder with sympathy – remembering how I had refused to give things away even when I moved to a much smaller bedroom… and then there was my stealing…

"It's okay," I said to the hoarder. "I see you."

The hoarder's eyes widened. "You… you do?"

It burst into bright blue light even before I touched it.

I'm getting better at this...

I could see how all of the fragments were fearful, and stuck in their own patterns, the way I sometimes got stuck on things… The more I could see it in myself the easier it became to absorb them.

Other faces rose to the top of the sludge-pile. There was the worried fragment from the Labyrinth.

"No, no, no!" they said, with hands over their eyes again.

I can definitely relate to this one...

I had dealt with anxiety so much that the empathy came easily to me for worry... I reached out, enveloping the fragment into another hug of brilliant bright light.

It was replaced with the angry raging face of the fiery fragment. I connected with my own rage at Felicity, at my parents, at life being unfair...

The fragment evaporated into the air even before I touched it, only to be replaced by the stubborn bull, which snorted at me.

I can be stubborn too... I realised... stubbornness comes from fear... just like judgement and most of these other things...

"It's okay," I said, and hugged the bull. It disappeared, just like the others, leaving me feeling even stronger.

The slug had shrunk in size... it was a much smaller wobbling mass of slime now. I kept going until there was just a lump, about the size of a beach ball.

I hugged it to my chest – it burst like a water balloon and I was left just holding the mirror with the purple frame.

Veila appeared at my side.

"You did it!"

"Veila!" I smiled at her. "Look!"

"Hey – it's the mirror!"

It was the mirror Honu had found at the bottom of the lake and that I had used to trap the fragments.

Last time I had looked at the mirror I had seen a different version of myself – stronger and braver, glowing, with different clothes.

I wiped away the slime and held the mirror up to look at myself – again I saw that different person – much stronger and braver, glowing much brighter, but still me.

"Why does it do that?" I asked Veila, "Why does it make me look different?"

Veila looked at me. "You do look different," she said.

I looked down and saw she was right. I was glowing, my clothing had changed and I was wearing the belt – just like the version of me the mirror had shown before…

It IS me…

It was just a very different me from the one I remembered.

"Is… is everyone okay?" I asked, looking around. I couldn't see much from the middle of the desert.

"I think so," Veila said. "Shall we go and check?"

It made sense to fly – to get to Honu and the Priestess Tree quickly. I had barely thought about flying when I realised I had already started hovering in mid-air like a superhero.

"Veila – look!" I called out, spinning around in the air. "I could never do this before – I could only take big jumps."

Veila laughed.

"Come on, let's go," she said.

We flew up over the Dreamrealm. I could see Honu in his lake as we flew over. He lifted his giant turtle arm and waved, and we waved back. We kept flying until we landed at the base of the Priestess Tree.

I looked back at the mess that was the dome, and the part of the forest that had been destroyed by the giant slug of fragments and felt guilty that I'd led them in there.

"It's okay, Dreamweaver," I heard a voice say. It sounded like the Priestess Tree but it wasn't just in my head this time.

I looked towards the tree and saw that it had transformed.

The Priestess from the roots of the tree had somehow come up, above the surface, and now appeared as if she was carved into the trunk.

"Hi!" I said. "What are you doing up here?"

"I just like a little sunshine on my skin now and then," said the Priestess Tree.

I didn't know if that was the real reason; I suspected she had come up to survey the damage I had caused.

"Don't feel guilty, Awa," the Priestess Tree said, looking at me. "You have done an amazing job– what you did in the Labyrinth to master the elements, and then to alchemise the fragments – you truly have surpassed all expectations… thank you for your courage and perseverance."

I blushed. I wasn't used to people saying such nice things about me.

"I can fly now," I said. "I can fly properly and... I look like I did the first time I saw myself in the mirror."

"The mirror will show you the attainment you seek," said the Priestess Tree, "whether you realise it or not."

"So that's why the fragments were so obsessed with it," I said. "They were seeing what they wanted to get."

"That's right, and now you have attained mastery," said the Priestess Tree. "It's fortunate that you've been able to master the elements so quickly – this will be necessary in the days to come."

Her voice became deeper and more serious as she spoke, hinting at danger.

"What do you mean?" I asked, "I already alchemised the fragments – the ones who have been attacking us."

"You have done much already," the Priestess Tree acknowledged. "However, the Shadow is much greater than any fragment can reflect – deeper and more terrifying..."

A shiver ran down my spine, chilling me to the bone.

"It's never over, is it?" I asked.

"There is always more!" said Veila, excitedly. "That's what keeps things interesting – remember."

I smiled at her as she flipped around in the air.

"But you may rest now," the Priestess Tree said, "or you may explore and play... You have many new abilities that you can try out. Where would you like to start?"

I thought about everything I had done in the

Dreamrealm and felt sad that it didn't connect with my waking life. I still couldn't even tell my friends about it without them thinking I'd gone nuts.

Unless...

I had an idea; I just didn't know if I'd be allowed to try it.

"What I really want to do is to see my friend Ella," I said. "Do you think it would be possible to visit her while she's dreaming?"

"Possible," said Veila, "certainly..."

"It is not without risk," said the Priestess Tree.

My heart sank in disappointment.

"But then, there is not much that can be accomplished without risk," the Priestess Tree continued.

"Do you mean, you'll let me?" I asked.

"We will not stand in your way," said the Priestess Tree.

"But you must take care," Veila added. "The humans are delicate in their dream state."

"I promise," I said, rubbing my hands together with excitement and accidentally sending tiny sparks of light out around me. "Oops... I might just have to get the hang of my new powers first!"

CHAPTER TWENTY-FIVE

I closed my eyes and stood there – in front of the large domed building of the Rooms of Mind where normal dreams happened. I knew that somehow every dreaming person was in there, but that they couldn't see each other... like they were each in their own dimension... and I just had to find one in particular.

I was thinking of Ella.

Use your intuition to find her, the Priestess Tree had said.

I pictured Ella in my head and remembered the feelings I associated with her, the colour yellow, her teddy bear collection, her smile.

I could sense her, somewhere in the Rooms of Mind, I knew that if I could just follow that feeling...

"I know where to go," I said to Veila.

"Have fun," Veila replied.

"Aren't you coming?"

"I think you'll give her enough of a surprise," Veila said, "A floating light creature might be a bit too much!"

"Okay," I said, smiling at my friend. "I'll see you soon."

I walked towards the main door to the building.

I entered what looked like a normal hallway, but I knew this was not at all ordinary!

I sensed that Ella was in here, somewhere, on the left. I walked down and turned left where it branched off.

I closed my eyes again.

I'm close.

I could sense a blue and yellow glowing light; that must be Ella. I opened my eyes in that direction and found the door.

I opened it to find…

A beach…

It was a bright sunny day. A familiar New Zealand beach spread out around me, with pale sand and rocks.

I decided to brighten the place up a bit – I knew the Rooms of Mind responded to our thoughts, so I thought: *the sand could be brighter, and the water could sparkle a bit more.* All the colours around me became more vivid.

I could see someone walking down the beach towards me.

I quickly shut the door and stepped in.

"Ella?" I called out.

"Oh… Awa," Ella said, coming towards me.

We both smiled.

"Isn't this beautiful?" she said. "How did you come to be here, in Napier?"

"Napier?"

"Yeah. This is where my family always holiday in the summer..."

Ella doesn't realise she's dreaming...

She had a kind of dazed look in her eyes, like Veila described dreaming humans often have.

I'm not going to tell her... but I'm sure we can have fun...

"I'm just visiting," I said. "Shall we go for a swim?"

Suddenly we were both wearing togs – although I'm not sure if it was something I did, or something Ella did, or was it just how the Rooms of Mind worked...?

"Yes!" Ella said, she grabbed my hand and we ran into the shallow waves.

We had fun, splashing around. It was so nice to be there, in Ella's dream, without a care in the world except...

Ella turned away and I saw a shimmer in the water a few metres away. I stepped closer, recognising the familiar face reflected in the water.

"Roimata," I whispered so that Ella couldn't hear, above the sounds of the ocean. "You're still alive. I thought..."

"Of course. Don't you see? You freed me!"

"I did?"

"Awa, we are all part of everything, and everything

is part of us – when we see this clearly, our fears lose their power over us. We are all connected..."

Roimata's face faded back into the water. I was relieved she was still alive – in some way – still connected to the water and... happy.

I turned back towards Ella and looked at her, still splashing happily in the water.

I still really want to tell her...

"Hey, Ella," I called out. "Look at this!"

I splashed the water towards her. Ella flinched but I flicked my wrists and moved the water back towards me. It hung in the air between us.

"Wow!" Ella gasped. "You're magic!"

She still had that slightly dazed look and I knew it would be an interesting dream.

I made more patterns in the water – making it swirl around into shapes, amazing Ella even more.

"Ella!" A voice broke through the sky.

"Ella, get up now! You'll be late for school!"

I was jolted awake to the sound of Ella's dad's voice.

I lay in bed, smiling after such a fun dream.

I didn't know if Ella would remember any of it – but I really wanted to find out!

As soon as I saw Ella in the school courtyard that morning, her eyes lit up.

"Oh my gosh, Awa! My dream!" she said. "It was amazing!"

"Really?" I said, trying to sound surprised. I wasn't quite ready to risk freaking Ella out.

"You were there – we were on a beach and you had magic water-bending powers!"

I smiled, knowing I was a little bit closer to being able to share my secret life with my friends.

The End

If you enjoyed this book, you can order Facing the Shadow: Dreamweavers Book 3.

(To be published August 2020.)

To hear all about the latest Dreamweavers updates, and get some cool giveaways, sign up to my mailing list! See my website on the following page.

ABOUT THE AUTHOR

Isa Pearl Ritchie is a New Zealand writer, based in Wellington. She has had many interesting dreams, including lucid dreams. She loves learning about people, society, and the way our minds work. She has completed a PhD in anthropology and a Masters in sociology. Her second novel, *Fishing for Māui,* was selected as one of the top books of 2018 in the New Zealand Listener and was a finalist in the NZ Booklovers Awards for Best Adult Fiction Book 2019. The *Dreamweavers* series are the first books she has written for young people.

www.isaritchie.com

facebook.com/isapearlritchie
twitter.com/isapearlritchie
instagram.com/isapearlritchie

ACKNOWLEDGMENTS

Many wonderful people have played an important part in the making of this book. Special thanks to *Active Sage* for the inspiration provided by your labyrinth, and for the image incorporated into the cover. Additional thanks to Jason Le Vaillant, Stephanie Joy Christie, Charles Barrie, Tesla Ritchie, and Cassie Hart, Ryn Richmond, and Dave Agnew, for your advice and support. Also a big thanks to all the test readers who gave such excellent feedback: Mira, Vidthia, Maddie, Lachlan Mead, and Joy Christlim Soriano.

Made in the USA
Las Vegas, NV
25 June 2022

50710343R00121